THE CONNEMARA
Champion

Ann Henning

U.S. DISTRIBUTOR
DUFOUR EDITIONS
CHESTER SPRINGS,
PA 19425-0007
(610) 458-5005

POOLBEG

Published in 1994 by
Poolbeg,
A division of Poolbeg Enterprises Ltd,
Knocksedan House,
123 Baldoyle Industrial Estate,
Dublin 13, Ireland

© Ann Henning 1994

The moral right of the author has been asserted.

The publishers gratefully acknowledge the assistance of
The Arts Council/An Chomhairle Ealaíon

A catalogue record for this book is available from the British Library.

ISBN 1 85371 335 X

Cover illustration by Don Conroy
Cover design by Poolbeg Group Services
Set by Poolbeg Group Services Ltd in Stone 10.5/14
Printed by The Guernsey Press Company Ltd,
Vale, Guernsey, Channel Islands

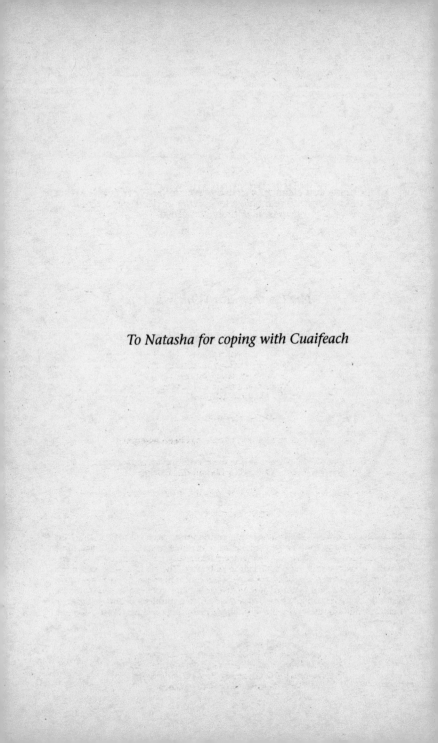

To Natasha for coping with Cuaifeach

By the same author

The Connemara Whirlwind

The Connemara Stallion

Contents

Critical Times

1

A man was hurrying up Main Street in Clifden, a little town in Connemara. It was called Main Street as opposed to Market Street, which was the other street in the town. The latter was by far the wider, to allow for stalls and stock on market days, and some contended that it was in fact the main street in the town, but never mind, the man was making his way up Main Street with all its shops, restaurants and public houses.

It was raining hard and a fair wind was blowing, but he did not seem to notice. His appearance indicated that he had spent some time out in the rain. His trousers were soaked and water ran in rivulets down the lapels of his black jacket—the top part of a lounge suit whose bottom had long since been discarded. The leather of his boots was darkened by mud and water. It was in fact remarkable that he had come out in such weather without being dressed for it. If there is one thing people in Connemara learn almost as soon as they are able to walk, it is to protect themselves against the elements.

The man stopped, first at one pub and then at another, for a brief glance inside. At Sweeney's, right at the top of the town where the Square joined the two streets together, he found what he was looking for and entered.

A few friends of his were gathered at the bar downing pints of beer bought for them by a late-season tourist who, in fair exchange, was being treated to snippets of information about this strange location where his holiday travels had suddenly come to a dead-end.

"Clifden Castle is a must," said one tall man answering to the name of Long John. "Nowhere in the world will you see a castle like it."

"Is that the hotel?" asked the tourist. "I saw it last night, beautifully lit up...."

The men snorted.

"The hotel! That one's no older than my youngest!"

"It looked quite ancient to me," the tourist insisted, but the men shook their heads, as much in denial as in disdain.

"It's a fake. The castle is something else altogether. The real thing. Nothing but ruins."

They were so engrossed in conversation they hadn't noticed Noel Walsh, the man who had just entered. But as he took a step towards them, they all reacted. The sight of his bare wet head, dark hair plastered over his forehead, water dripping steadily off the tip of his big nose, was enough to reveal that something was seriously wrong.

"Noel Walsh! Whatever happened to your hat?" Long John exclaimed, as if the absence of his hat was somehow at the core of his troubles. The others felt much the same, used as they were to seeing him crowned with a tweed trilby, faded and crumpled and slightly shrunk by years of battering by the Connemara weather. But the hat had little to do with Noel's problems, except that he had been so preoccupied when he left home, he had forgotten to put it on.

At first he said nothing, just sank down limply on a barstool. Long John made a discreet gesture to the barman to tend to his needs, which were only too obvious. When Noel finally spoke, his voice sounded strangely flat.

"He came to see me today."

"Who for God's sake?" demanded another man called Paddy Pat. "Listening to you, you'd think it was the divil himself had paid you a visit."

Noel gave him a glance to suggest that this wasn't far out. Then, after heaving a deep sigh, he said in a somewhat steadier voice, "The man from the Department."

There was a deep silence. The men frowned. For the past few weeks they had heard rumours about a man from the Department of Agriculture going round South Connemara, singling out certain owners of Connemara ponies and subjecting them to a highly intrusive interrogation. He professed to be conducting a survey, but nobody believed this to be true. In Connemara nobody believed a word uttered by a person acting in an official capacity.

"What was he like?" one of the men wanted to know.

"Oh, you know the type, a right snob, wearing a suit and tie in the middle of the week and a pink shirt, of all things, to go with it!"

"Never mind what he looked like," Long John cut him off impatiently. "What was he after? Did he tell you that?"

"He just kept asking me these questions," Noel said, his voice echoing the exasperation he had felt when faced with the onslaught from the official. "Questions about the ponies, how many I had, how many I'd sold, who bought them, how much I got for them...."

"That sounds like real bad news to me," Paddy Pat stated sombrely.

"What beats me," said Long John, "is why he pretends to be from the Department, when anyone but a blind bat can see he's a taxman."

At that the others had to take deep fortifying draughts from their pints.

"Why are you so worried about the taxman?" the tourist asked, displeased that the conversation had steered a long way away from the useful tourist information that would obviously cost him dearly, whether it was delivered or not.

The men stared at him as if they couldn't make head or tail of his question. But then Long John, tactful as ever, came to the rescue.

"I don't know what matters be like in your country," he began, "but in this part of the world...." He paused for effect. "Taxmen have no shame."

"There was this poor old man came back from America," Paddy Pat told him eagerly. "All his life he had worked hard, breaking his back on the building sites in Boston. He brought back his life savings, which wasn't much, God knows, just enough to see him through his old age and pay the funeral expenses.... He kept the money well hidden in his mattress."

"His mattress?" the tourist said scornfully. "You mean that kind of thing still goes on here?"

"Well he said himself that he didn't think anyone would believe him stupid enough to keep it there, so he reckoned it would be a safe enough place for it," Paddy Pat continued. "But he hadn't counted on the taxman being so cute. I suppose you have to be real sly to land a job like that," he finished disparagingly.

"Half his money they took," Long John added in a voice full of outrage and went on, as no sound of agreement issued from the tourist. "I mean, it wasn't as if he hadn't worked for his money. It had taken him a lifetime of hard labour, and they didn't even leave him enough for a decent wake. It was a downright scandal."

"So it was," the other men assented, aggrieved at the thought of the good wake they were going to miss. "A downright scandal, so it was."

The tourist's upper lip was curling in a way that

did not betray much sympathy. "Of course he should pay his tax," he said. "Everyone should pay his tax. In my country, Sweden that is," he added proudly, "we regard it as an honour for each citizen to contribute to the welfare of the nation. It's what gives a man his dignity."

Noel Walsh spluttered on his Guinness. This was too much for him to swallow in his present frame of mind. "I'd heard some of them foreigners were barking mad," he muttered. "But I didn't realise it went to such lengths."

Once more Long John's talents at diplomacy were called upon. "They have a different lifestyle over there," he said placatingly to his friends, and then turned to the tourist. "Isn't that so?"

The Swede nodded approvingly, and Long John continued: "We might all be the same if we did nothing all day but ski."

"Ski?" the Swede repeated, baffled.

"Nothing but Alps, isn't it?"

Long John had done well at national school and liked to show off whenever an opportunity presented itself.

"I'm from Sweden, not Switzerland," said the tourist condescendingly.

Long John shrugged it off. "Oh well, it's all the same. Freezing cold, anyhow. That's what gets to them," he concluded, once more addressing his friends.

Then, sensing that the tourist still needed convincing about the general duplicity of Irish people in a position of authority, they went on to entertain him with the touching story of Bertie Nee, a story that had gone round Connemara all summer and still pleased everyone to hear. Bertie was what you might call a mature bachelor who only recently had taken over the small family farm from his elderly father. Everyone knew that he was desperate to find himself a wife, but so far he had been unsuccessful, mainly because, according to the men, "he set his aim too high". The few women who were considered good enough for him expected something other than Bertie Nee for a husband. However, nursing the illusion that his charm would one day make up for the scarcity of what he had to offer, Bertie relentlessly pursued any classy woman he could spot, preferably strangers to the area whom he reckoned would be more susceptible and less prejudiced against him.

So it was that one sunny spring morning when he was on his way out to the fields to feed his cattle, an expensive-looking car drove up and a most attractive young woman stuck her head out to ask him the way to Streamstown. Bertie made the most of this God-sent occasion, pointed out the lovely views over the sea and even got her to step out of her car to come and admire them with him.

"Is this all your land?" she asked him. "What handsome cows! Do you have many of them?"

Bertie told her he was the owner of the best land in Connemara and the finest stock to go with it. He took it as a good sign that she wanted to know how many animals he possessed and did his best to impress her, trebling the number of cattle and sheep just to reassure her before asking her out for a drink that evening.

"You must be making a lot of money, so," she mused. Bertie conceded that he wasn't exactly short of a penny or two. In fact, he confided, he was much better off than anyone gave him credit for. This last he added just in case she came across some envious local person who might inform her to the contrary.

Even so, she sweetly declined his offer of a drink, saying she had to get back to her office in Galway. Bertie was pleased to learn that she had a job, and therewith income of her own.

"Do let me take your telephone number," he pleaded, looking her deep in the eyes.

"There's no need," she replied, a hint of a smile in her voice. "You'll be hearing from me."

And he did. The woman turned out to be an inspector from the Department of Social Welfare out to check on people who exceeded their permitted quota of livestock whilst at the same time claiming unemployment benefit. Bertie had got into terrible trouble: his dole had been withdrawn straight away and it had proved near enough impossible to convince the authorities that he didn't have more animals than he actually did.

"Sly and cute they are" was Paddy Pat's final comment.

The Swedish tourist, having been presented with the bill and seeing that the glasses were drawing alarmingly close to a refill, quickly withdrew at this point, whereupon the talk centred on the direction in which the man from the Department had last been seen heading.

"I'm damned if I know," said Noel Walsh. "The worst of it is, he doesn't go to everyone. I just wish I knew what I have done to deserve being picked upon."

"Sly and cute," Paddy Pat reiterated.

***

Tom and Doreen Joyce, teenage brother and sister, were walking home one afternoon when they discovered a big black car parked right in the middle of the narrow causeway that connected Inishnee with the mainland.

"What kind of eejit would leave his car there?" said Tom. "Sure he's stopping everyone else from going both to and from the island. Ah," he added as they got closer, "it's got a Dublin plate," as if this was sufficient explanation.

The car, it turned out, hadn't been left there. A man was sitting inside, and at the sound of their footsteps on the causeway he got out, a tall, thin man with a despairing look on his face.

"I seem to have run out of petrol," he told them. "In such an awkward spot, too. Would you be kind enough to help me get the car off the road?"

Tom and Doreen pushed, while he steered the car off the causeway, onto a patch of grass just where the island began.

"There's a garage not far away," Tom told him. "You can get petrol there."

"Oh thank goodness," said the man, jumping out of the car so fast he got his leg caught in the seat-belt and narrowly missed falling flat on his face. "If you tell me where it is, I'll start walking straight away."

Tom glanced at the man's thin shoes, more suited to city streets than to a hike across Connemara bogland. "I'll go," he offered. "It will be quicker that way."

The man, obviously relieved and immensely grateful, produced an empty can from the boot and then pulled out a ten pound note from his pocket. "This is for petrol," he said to Tom, "and this," he pulled out another note, "is for you. For the trouble," he added when Tom did not take it.

"Never you mind," said Tom, who had been brought up never to accept money for something he himself regarded as a favour. "I'll be back in half an hour, so."

As he departed, the man asked Doreen to hold on while he rooted around in the car and located a thick file. "I may be able to use this time fruitfully," he said, rummaging amongst a sheaf of papers. "Tell me, do you know of someone called...let's see...Doreen Joyce?"

"Doreen Joyce? But that's me!" the girl said, astonished.

The man looked equally taken aback. "Could there be another person with that name?" he asked.

"According to my notes, Doreen Joyce is the registered owner of a Connemara pony stallion."

"That's right. I have a stallion. Cuaifeach."

"Really?" The man, for some reason, sounded quite pleased. "In that case," he went on, "I'd like to ask you a few questions."

"Why?" Doreen wanted to know. "What do you want to ask me questions for?"

"It's for a survey," the man explained in the tired voice of someone who has had to say the same thing a hundred times over. "I'm from the Department of Agriculture. We just want to find out a little more about the ponies in Connemara."

"You better speak to my dad," the girl told him.

"No, no," the man said quickly, as if this was the last thing he wanted. "I'm sure you'll be able to tell me all I want to know. If you're fit to keep a stallion...." He gave her a wink and a nod.

Oh well, Doreen thought, he can't make me say anything I don't want to tell him.

The man started searching through his file again. With his short-cropped brown hair and horn-rimmed spectacles he looked very strict, a bit like the politicians you see interviewed on television, Doreen reflected. The questions he went on to ask made no sense to her at all, but she couldn't see that answering them could do any harm. First of all, he wanted to know how many ponies she kept. Well that was easy, it was only the one, and he knew about Cuaifeach already.

"One, but a lion," said the man with a smile,

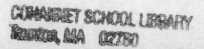

leaning over the bonnet of the car whilst noting something down on his form.

Doreen looked at him blankly.

"Haven't you heard that old fable?" the man asked. "The vixen taunted the lioness for having only one cub, when she herself had six. And the lioness replied, 'One, but a lion.'"

Doreen laughed. "That's a fair description of Cuaifeach."

Had she no broodmares, no youngstock? No. How many ponies did she have five years ago?

"None. Five years ago I was only ten."

"And three years ago?"

"Three years ago?" The girl reflected. "Then I was just after buying Cuaifeach."

Doreen sighed. It had been three long years. Not that she regretted any of them, but it certainly hadn't been easy. It still wasn't.

"In what conditions is he kept?" the man wondered.

"I'm well able to look after him, if that's what you mean," Doreen replied defensively.

"I don't mean anything," the man assured her. "I am merely asking questions for the purpose of the survey."

"He's looked after by a friend of mine," said Doreen. "Over at Errislannan. It's close to the pony club."

"Oh? He's broken and riding?" The man, suddenly more interested, started scribbling on his form. "Do you ride him yourself?"

"After a fashion," said Doreen, afraid that he'd want to go into more detail, but he didn't. A number of questions that followed related to broodmares and youngstock and so obviously did not apply to her, he said, neatly printing NA in the margin of the form. But then he asked, somewhat abruptly, "Do you have any intention of selling him?"

Doreen's reaction was like that of a hedgehog prodded with a stick. "Is that why you're here?" she said, not even trying to conceal her prickles.

The man waved his hand disarmingly. "Certainly not, my dear girl! I keep telling you, I am only here to ask questions."

"Well he's not for sale," Doreen stated doggedly. "I've said it before, and I'll say it again. I wouldn't part with him for all the money in the world."

This information seemed to be of no value to the man; nothing was written down on the form. He just glanced at it and asked casually, "Any idea as to what he might be worth?"

"I don't know," said Doreen. "I don't know and I don't care. What does it matter when I'm not selling him anyway?"

At this point a sharp gust of wind found its way into the folder which the man, unwisely, had left open on the bonnet of his car. A pile of completed forms lifted in the air and scattered all around them. With a cry of dismay, the man leaped up to try and catch them before they hit the muddy ground. The way he jumped about flapping his arms reminded

Doreen of some big bird engaged in a ritual mating dance. She did her best to help him, feeling a little sorry for this tall man who, in spite of his strict appearance, seemed to have little luck in his dealings with the more practical aspects of life.

"Thank you so much," he panted, dabbing furiously with his handkerchief at the forms that they hadn't been able to catch in time. "You have no idea what it has cost me to get this information together in the first place...."

"Are you done questioning me?" Doreen wondered.

"Let me see...." He thumbed through his papers again. "Not quite. I'd like to know approximately how much you spend on the pony's keep. Feed, bedding, veterinary charges, that kind of thing. The annual figure?"

"I haven't a clue," said Doreen. "You'd want to ask Mrs O'Reilly about that. She's the one that keeps the stallion for me, and she pays all the expenses in return for having him run with her mares."

"Oh, she has broodmares?" the man said keenly. "Perhaps I could interview her next?"

Doreen hesitated.

"Would she mind? Is she one of these obstinate people who press their lips together and seal them with wax when you ask them a question?"

"Most of the people I know," Doreen said with a smile, "would skin me alive for sending the likes of you onto them."

The man threw up his hands and was just about to embark on an agitated speech, but Doreen cut him short.

"Not Mrs O'Reilly, though. She is different."

2

There was a loud noise as two heavy timbers fell to the ground. Julia rushed to the nearest window and looked out to see a man in a grey suit letting himself in through the gate. It appeared he had accidentally knocked down its carefully devised superstructure, two thick wooden bars acting as a barricade to stop Cuaifeach from jumping out onto the road. She rushed out to warn him but it was too late. The stallion, equally alerted by the heavy thuds, had already galloped up to the gate. Right in front of the visitor he stopped short, as if to thank him for the favour. The man, alarmed at the sight of the wildly excited animal, took a step back, tripped on one of the timbers and fell backwards in the mud. Cuaifeach, never one to miss a good opportunity, disappeared in a flash through the open gate.

"Oh no!" Julia wailed. "Not again!"

The garden, with its high stone walls and fuchsia hedges, was the only place where she could safely let the stallion out for a few hours of supervised grazing every day. Cuaifeach did not believe in the constraints necessarily imposed on stallions. No field had fences high enough to contain him, and mare owners in the area were, understandably, very sensitive about his unwarranted visits. Julia had already received several stern warnings. Only a couple of days ago, one person had even threatened to report her, if the stallion got out once more. She had promised him, as well as herself, that it would never happen again and had indeed taken every precaution to ensure that it wouldn't.

She ran back into the house, grabbed the head-collar she kept by the front door for emergencies such as this, and took up the pursuit, paying scant attention to the man who had just picked himself up off the ground and, with a highly concerned expression, was examining the damage done to his suit.

Cuaifeach was already a good way off in the distance, and Julia set off after him with a sinking feeling in her stomach. She knew that her chances of catching him were slim. He would stop eventually, but the question was where, on whose land. The more sympathetic neighbours would help by herding him into a safe place, luring him with titbits or armfuls of hay. But then there were other places, where he was less than welcome.

As long as he didn't take himself off onto Jim Lydon's land.... This man had some lovely show ponies and took his breeding programme seriously to say the least. Julia had no doubt that he would carry out his threat and contact the authorities, if he saw the stallion out again. And since Jim Lydon had one of the largest farms in the area, with huge tracts of land stretching in all directions, it was more likely than not that Cuaifeach would end up once more in one of his fields.

She could see him as a dark moving spot against the rough ground, faded in muted colours now in late autum under a grey overcast sky. Julia looked out over the landscape with a feeling of utter helplessness. Much as she loved the wide open spaces, at times such as these when her own urgent wishes were pitched against them, she knew that they could, and would, always defeat her.

A shiny black car had driven up behind her. The man in the grey suit got out.

"I'm most awfully sorry," he began. "I should have known better...."

Julia still had her eyes on the stallion. "You filthy beast," she hissed between clenched teeth. "Don't you even think about it!"

The man looked her up and down in a very strange way.

"He mustn't go up there!" she cried. "That land belongs to a man called Jim Lydon and he...." She stopped herself. There was no need to go into any detail.

"You get into my car," the man suggested mildly, as if she, too, was some wild thing that might do something dangerous if provoked. "We may be able to cut across and stop him."

Only after she had seated herself in the passenger

seat and they had started off did she turn to look at the man. Then it was her turn to stare. Stare at the fine features, the horn-rimmed spectacles, the petulant expression around the mouth that would suddenly dissolve into a smile.

"Wilfrid!" she exclaimed. "I can't believe it!"

In a moment she had forgotten all about escaping stallions. She was back in England, back in Cirencester, back many years to the days when she had still lived at home with her parents. That was when she had last seen Wilfrid Smith-Andrews. He had been a student at the agricultural college and one of her most ardent young suitors.

"Julia," Wilfrid said softly. "I thought it was you. Only, your manner has changed somewhat."

"Whatever brought you here?" she asked him.

He didn't hear her question. "You married," he reminded himself. "You married Eric O'Reilly."

"Yes," Julia replied in a low voice. "I married Eric. But he died."

"I know," Wilfrid said. "I thought of you at the time. I'm sorry."

In the silence that followed, Julia suddenly remembered Cuaifeach. "Take this track to the left," she directed him.

It was a small boreen winding its way around rocks and bog-holes. The stallion was nowhere in sight. Soon they would arrive at Jim Lydon's homestead, and what would happen there Julia would rather not think about. But then, as they came round a big bend, they discovered a battered blue car blocking the track. Next to it was its owner casually holding out a black bucket, and out of it Cuaifeach was munching away greedily.

"Johnny Tass!" Julia called out, relieved, as she got out of the car. "Am I glad to see you! Whatever brought you here?"

Johnny, modest as ever, told her he had been on his way back after visiting Jim Lydon. To hear the latest gossip he told her, winking. He was a man drawn to gossip as irresistibly as a thirsty horse to water.

"Jim doesn't strike me as a gossipy type," Julia remarked, but Johnny Tass disagreed.

"He hasn't a good thing to say about anyone, and especially behind their backs!" However, the main reason for his visit had been to inform Johnny that the man from the Department was drawing near. "I hope you're planning a visit up there," he said to Wilfrid, who had got out to join them. "He told me he has a word or two to spare for dim-witted officials who stick their noses where they have no business!"

"Don't mind him," Julia said quickly, worried that Wilfrid might take offence. "He always goes on like this."

"And he said he was going to lodge a complaint," Johnny continued gleefully, "about the ignorant Englishwoman who shouldn't be allowed to keep a stallion she can't control. Was I glad to catch this fellow!" he added with a wink in Julia's direction. "You know I like you much better than that old stick-in-the-mud."

"Oh Johnny," Julia said, "I can never thank you enough."

Whilst they talked, Julia had caught Cuaifeach who, with his head deep in Johnny's bucket, seemed more intent on oats than on his highly priced liberty. The bucket was then duly restored to the boot of Johnny's car, a virtual goldmine of useful aids. Lengths of rope, a sledgehammer, rolls of wire fencing, bags of feedstuffs, sheep-shears, syringes of worm paste, even a pincer-like instrument used for castrating bulls, plus a few other odds and ends that might come in handy in the daily life of a true Connemara fixer.

Julia said goodbye to Johnny and started to walk the stallion back.

"I'll meet you at the house," Wilfrid said eagerly. "And then, perhaps, you'll let me bother you with a few simple questions?"

***

"Sometimes I feel I could tear my hair out."

Wilfrid, comfortably settled on Julia's sofa and enjoying a nice cup of tea, was in the process of telling her about the problems of conducting a survey in Connemara. People were being very difficult, no-one would give him a straight answer, he was met by suspicion if not downright defiance. "You'd think I was an enemy out for their blood!" he complained. "I mean, it's not as if I'm acting in anything but their own interest. They need help desperately, if Connemara is not to lose its ponies altogether!"

"Why would they lose their ponies?" Julia asked.

Wilfrid explained. A severe crisis was facing the ponies in this region. Numbers were going down at an alarming rate, land was given over to cattle and sheep, which, with generous EC grants, were proving much more profitable. The best mares were being sold for peanuts out of Connemara, just to be got rid of. Families who had kept ponies for generations were getting out of them since they were unable to afford the luxury of wasting so much valuable grazing on animals that brought in comparatively little in return.

"Last year only one out of every three Connemaras registered in this country was resident in Connemara, and the trend keeps going down."

"That's terrible," Julia said. "After all, there's no better place for young Connemara ponies. This is where they originated, the only place where their best characteristics develop freely."

Even after three years in Connemara, she never ceased to be amazed at the way the native ponies thrived on the meagre grazing and the rough land, conditions in which other horses would be hard put to even survive. Foals jumped walls and climbed mountains as soon as they were born, growing into the agile, hardy little animals that the world knew as Connemara ponies.

"I've seen Connemaras bred in England and other parts of the world," she said to Wilfrid. "They haven't got a stitch on the ones reared over here."

"I know," he replied. "But if the present trend continues, there will be no ponies left in Connemara in years to come. And research has shown that once a species is lost to an area, it's near enough impossible to bring it back."

The purpose of his survey, he continued, was to pinpoint the reasons for the decline, so that the government could institute measures to reverse the trend before it was too late.

Julia pondered this for a moment. Then she said, "I believed somehow that I was the only one having difficulties. You know, being a blow-in and all...."

"Blow-ins" was the term used in Connemara for outsiders who "blew in" on an easterly wind and then, likely as not, blew out again before long.

"But now, listening to you, I realise that it's much more serious than that."

"So what's your experience?" Wilfrid asked, delighted at last to have found someone who would give an open and candid report on the conditions he was appointed to survey.

Julia told him about the high-flying hopes she had had when she bought her three broodmares, selecting the best she could find, and putting them to a stallion of well-proven champion blood. The result this first year had been three gorgeous foals, a better return than she had expected. Only they were all colts, and now that they were weaned and ready to sell, she couldn't find a buyer for them.

"Have you tried?" asked Wilfrid, scribbling on his pad.

"I took them to the fair at Maam Cross last week. That, I am told, is the main outlet here for foals. But the few offers I received weren't even worth considering. They wouldn't have covered my costs."

"How much were you offered?"

"The top bid was five hundred pounds for the three. They'd go to meat at that; I couldn't even consider it. What really kills me," she burst out vehemently, "is knowing how much riding ponies like these fetch on the international market. The world is full of people prepared to pay high prices for top-quality Connemaras. Given the right place and customer, my foals would be worth ten times what I was offered at Maam Cross."

Wilfrid nodded. "The lack of a direct link between producer and consumer is definitely one important aspect of the problem."

"There must be a number of dealers along the line," Julia resumed, "picking up handsome profits. People who haven't done a thing to deserve it. If it wasn't for them, breeders here would get more for their youngstock, enough anyhow to make it worth their while to go on breeding their lovely ponies."

"Your best bet," Wilfrid advised her, "would be to market your colts yourself directly to the overseas market. Surely, with your contacts, you should be able to find someone in England."

Julia agreed. She'd already thought of that option. It would mean extra work, time taken away from her painting, but she really had no choice in the matter. She didn't have the facilities to keep three colts through the winter, and she already had enough problems, surrounded as she was by the likes of Jim Lydon. On top of it all, the foals showed every sign of having inherited their father's exuberant, wilful nature, characteristics that would serve them well as performance ponies but made them more of a handful to rear.

"I'll do just that," she said. "It's my only option. But what about all the other local breeders facing the same problem? What do you propose to do to improve their lot?"

Wilfrid, not being a civil servant for nothing, stated that the primary objective was to get enough hard facts down on paper. That in itself would take time, given the general lack of co-operation afforded by the pony owners. However, once that was accomplished, he could get down to analysing the results of his survey and report back to his department. It would then be up to his superiors to call upon the government to act upon the findings.

"So what will they do?" Julia asked, reflecting that by then it might well be too late. For each good broodmare that left Connemara, the area was left that much poorer.

"I suppose they'll find a way to extend the EC grants to include ponies. Grants for foals, for example, would be an incentive for breeders to hold on to their mares."

"What good would that be," Julia protested, "if people can't sell the foals they breed? With more ponies, and a continually weak market, prices will drop even further! Wouldn't it be better to help the breeders sell their youngstock at adequate prices? For a start you could cut out the middlemen."

Wilfrid flinched slightly. "My dear Julia, that's not my task. The measures to be taken will all depend on the views of the government of the day."

He paused and sipped his tea, glancing furtively at Julia, thinking how lovely she looked when she was agitated, it brought light and sparkle to her face. Once, years ago, he had seen her look like that...in her parents' garden in Cirencester...the time when he had tried to kiss her. Would he ever get a second chance, he wondered. If he did, would her reaction be the same? After all, they were both unattached now.

A loud bang outside made him jump. Half the contents of his teacup spilled down his pink shirt front. Julia tried not to laugh, thinking to herself that, whatever the intervening years had done to Wilfrid, they hadn't made him any less clumsy than he used to be. It was a trait she had always found somehow endearing, but in the interests of all concerned, it was probably as well that he had given up his ambitions to become a farmer and instead had settled for the civil service.

"It's only Cuaifeach," she explained, handing him a napkin, "reminding me that his tea is due. It's a terrible habit he has, kicking his stable door on the dot of five. I don't know how to stop it."

Wilfrid shook his head as he dried his wet chest with the napkin. "That stallion," he muttered, going on to brush some of the mud off his trouser-leg. "Isn't he more trouble than he's worth?"

Julia shrugged. Cuaifeach's stud career had been far from successful. Local breeders seemed to share the view of the neighbouring old man she had approached with an offer of stallion service. He had been outraged, as if she had tried to force some delinquent youth onto his teenage daughter.

"That hooligan!" he had exclaimed. "I wouldn't let him near my little Katie. Don't you know, he'd kill her dead!"

Julia, who had had Cuaifeach cover her own three mares and had been surprised to witness the kindness, even tenderness, displayed by the stallion in amorous encounters, assured the old man that he had nothing to worry about. Cuaifeach was a perfect gentleman, and all the mares adored him.

But the man shook his head. "Even if that were so," he said, "what would be coming out of her next spring? Another one like him? No thanks, I'll be taking my Katie over to Jackie's, as usual."

Added to the breeders' ingrained fear of producing "bad blood" was the unfortunate circumstance that, so far, Cuaifeach had thrown only colts. That had finally and decisively put him on the breeders' black list. When Julia advertised his services in the *Farmers' Journal,* she hadn't had a single taker.

"I'm beginning to think they are all more trouble than they're worth," she said dejectedly. "The sooner I find an overseas buyer, the better. The way things are, no-one here can afford the luxury of being a pony owner."

Wilfrid smiled indulgently. "That, my dear, is the very situation I've been appointed to ameliorate."

Julia gave him a doubtful look. For all his theories and good intentions, the Wilfrid she knew wasn't noted for his practical achievements. If the future of the Connemara pony rested or fell with him, it did indeed look gloomy.

3

"Hi there! How is life in Connemara?" Doreen looked up, delighted to see that her friend Dominic O'Neill had come back for his Christmas holidays. He was mounted on Rosie, the mare his father had bought him and kept especially for his visits to Connemara. Cuaifeach, too, was pleased to see an old friend. He started sniffing Rosie all over, pawing the ground excitedly.

"Pretty dull," she replied, noting that Dominic had grown since the summer. He was really too tall now for his pony. As always he looked very nice; he was wearing a tan tweed hacking jacket with a matching polo, maroon breeches and black leather boots. You could be forgiven for thinking he was on his way to a fashion parade, not a riding lesson. "You know there's nothing much happening here in winter."

"Cuaifeach looks great. Has he been to any more shows?"

"Dominic!" she cried. "Don't be reminding me of the shows! It's not fair."

Dominic grinned. While he had had a reasonably successful show season with Rosie, it had been a disaster for Doreen. Having worked very hard all winter and spring to prepare her pony for the summer's riding classes, she had eventually got him going really well. But the minute he entered a show ring, Cuaifeach decided to apply his own outrageous standards for showing himself off. He seemed to think that the only thing that mattered was catching the eye of the judges, and this he achieved admirably by galloping like a lunatic around the ring when he was meant to stand still; pulling himself up in a perfect stance, dead square, not moving as much as a hair when he was supposed to gallop; doing an advanced half pass across the ring when the instruction was to go in a straight line, and bucking exuberantly when asked to extend his trot.

The judges certainly couldn't fail to take notice, but his powerful physique and beautiful paces cut no ice when it came to the final line-up. The best he had managed, on a comparatively good day and with a sympathetic judge, had been a fourth in a class of six.

It was not that Doreen was a bad loser. In Cuaifeach's first season when he was only four, she had entered him in the show classes not expecting to win. Knowing that he wasn't ready and telling herself that he was really only there to gain experience, she had gladly accepted ending up at the bottom end of the line. But the following year had been different. She had been so sure that he had all it took to sweep the board, and according to some judges, he would have, had he only behaved a little better. But they couldn't possibly award such an ill-mannered pony; it wouldn't be fair on the other contestants who, though often inferior, at least did everything right. Doreen understood, but that made it somehow even more heart-breaking. For each new show she entered she had pleaded with her stallion, threatened and bargained with him, to get him to put on his best behaviour—but to no avail. He let her down unfailingly, time and time again. His performances became notorious as the season went on, causing much mirth amongst competitors and spectators. Only Doreen was not amused.

"How have you been yourself?" she asked Dominic, to get off the depressing subject of shows.

"Great," he said, blue eyes glittering. "I've got into showjumping in a big way. There'll be no more of these sissy show classes for me."

"Oh." Doreen felt at once sad and relieved that there would be no more challenging encounters with Dominic and Rosie next summer. "Have you been in competitions and all?"

"Every Sunday," he replied proudly. "I have this really cool instructor who used to be on the Irish team. He says I have a grand eye for a stride."

"That's marvellous," said Doreen, though she didn't know quite what this meant.

"All I need now is good jumping pony. Rosie is useless over fences and, besides, she's too small."

As he said this, Rosie gave a loud snort, sounding

very offended.

They both laughed.

"Surely your dad will fix you up," Doreen said, regretting her words the same instant. She didn't want to sound envious, but sometimes it was difficult to have a friend whose father was a millionaire, when your own was unemployed for much of the time.

Dominic pulled a face. "My dad is funny that way. He doesn't mind what he pays for expenses, like registration fees and gear and lessons. But when it comes to buying a pony, he's real mean. He can't seem to get it into his head that ponies worth having cost money."

"How much would you have to pay for a good jumping pony?" Doreen asked.

"All the ones I've seen cost around ten thousand."

"Ten thousand!" she cried. "In that case I must say I don't blame your dad."

"I tell him there's no point getting anything but the best. It's not as if he couldn't afford it. But he says, before he spends that kind of money, I shall have to prove myself worthy of it. But how can I prove myself when I never get to ride anything halfway decent? I have to make do with ropy old ponies from the riding-school."

Doreen tried to look sympathetic, but couldn't find it in her heart to feel all that sorry for him.

They were part of a group of ponies and riders that had gathered at the entrance to O'Briens' Equestrian Centre at Murvey. From having started out as a rough trekking outfit, the O'Brien brothers had expanded, thanks to generous grants from the Tourist Board and liberal cash injections from their neighbour, Olympic swimming star Roc O'Neill, who had decided to include their operation in his luxurious leisure centure. They now even sported an international size riding arena, and in order to make use of it during the otherwise quiet winter season, they were offering "Christmas holiday riding clinics with one of Ireland's top instructors". This was the first of three, and they had had eighteen takers, mainly members of the Clifden pony club.

The instructor had come out and was walking towards the arena. She waved to the group to join her. It was a dull and breezy morning, and both riders and ponies were glad to start moving and get the December chill out of their bones. Cuaifeach was particularly keen, as always, at the prospect of something happening. That was something he could never get enough of.

Dominic looked the stallion up and down as they walked along the track. "Have you ever thought of trying him over jumps, Doreen? There are lots of good showjumping Connemara stallions, I know of several Grade A."

"He's doing quite enough of that sort of thing already," said Doreen. "There's not a fence in the country that's too high for him."

"Really?" said Dominic enthusiastically. "He'd be a great one for hunting, so. Did you ever take him hunting, Doreen?"

"Sure," she replied airily.

"Where?" he wanted to know. "With whom, what pack? How many times have you been out?"

"We hunt rabbits at Dunloughan," she said. "Come off it, Dominic, you're not on the east coast now. You know as well as I do that there's no hunting in Connemara. No showjumping either, for that matter."

The "top instructor" advertised by the O'Briens was a short, stout girl from Dublin, supplied by an agency for equestrian staff. She had landed this employment on the strength of good references from her former employers which described her as "a robust, competent instructor, sharp and capable, well qualified, setting her standards high". What they hadn't mentioned was the fact that she had made herself rather unpopular in most places, owing to her tendency to favour some pupils and pick on others, for no apparent reason.

"Right!" she called in a booming voice, trained to carry above the thudding of many hooves and high Irish winds, "Let's get these ponies moving! Make them go forward, push them on from behind! They all look as if they're half asleep!"

Cracking the lunge-whip she was carrying, she let her eyes wander around the ring searching for ponies on whom she could concentrate her teaching efforts. It was her method of working; she didn't believe in giving each the same amount of attention, "spreading herself too thinly," as she herself termed it.

What she saw was a mass of dappled grey ponies

ridden by teenage girls, all looking more or less the same to her. But one equipage stood out, a classy chestnut, ridden by a well turned-out boy. She smiled. That was the sort of thing she liked to see.

"You take up leading file!" she directed him. "Whole ride, trot on!"

As the ride trotted, she called out instructions to improve the riders' positions: to look straight ahead, keep their heels down, shoulders back, legs on, a good contact with the reins. Always the same wherever she went, she reflected with a pang of boredom. She might as well bring along a gramophone record and play it to them while she herself went for an extended coffee break. Oh, why had she chosen to be a riding instructor? It really was a tedious job.

Then she spotted a bay pony at the end of the ride lagging behind the others; there was a gap of at least four lengths between him and the rider in front. That cheered her up a bit.

"Push him on!" she shouted to the girl riding him. "Don't just sit there like a turnip! You're here to work!"

She told leading file to canter to the end of the ride, which he did in an exemplary fashion, earning himself a benign nod of approval. The other ponies followed suit, one after the other, more or less willingly. But when it was the turn of the bay pony, he wouldn't canter at all.

"Go on!" she boomed. "Ask him again, in the corner this time! Put your legs on, for God's sake, you're not sitting in an armchair! Use your stick! Give him a good wallop!"

"I haven't got a stick!" Doreen called back. "Sticks don't work with him, they make him buck."

"Nonsense," said the instructor. She took a riding-crop from one of the other riders and held it out to Doreen, but she declined to take it.

"It's no good," she insisted.

The instructor shook her head, obviously annoyed. "All right then, you just have to rely on your legs. Come on, give with your hands and use those legs; what do you think they are for? Give with your hands, I said! How can you expect him to go forward when you're holding him back? It's like giving gas when you have the handbrake on!"

Doreen did her best to follow the orders, but did not get much help from Cuaifeach, who was giving every sign of having "one of his days". The instructor raised her lunge-whip.

"Go on!" she bellowed. "Canter!"

The whip landed on Cuaifeach's hind quarters and as a result he completed some fifteen loops of the school at a flat out gallop. There was one moment when he was going straight at the instructor and she had to jump out of his path. She looked furtively over her shoulder to check if anyone had noticed the startled look on her face. When Doreen finally managed to steer her stallion back to his place at the end of the ride, he very nearly crashed into the pony in front of him. Once he had settled back into a trot, he looked proudly back at the instructor as if wanting to say, that good enough for you? She chose to ignore him.

Leading file was told to change the rein across the school and repeat the exercise on the other rein. One by one the riders were given the order to canter on, which they all did without incident. The instructor did not pay them much attention; she was saving herself up to have another go at Cuaifeach.

"Very well," she said, raising the lunge-whip once more, a glint of malicious excitement in her eye. "This time, at least make an attempt to control your pony!"

Cuaifeach performed a faultless controlled canter around the school. He went on the bit, extended his stride beautifully, and let himself be brought back to a trot just at the right moment. The instructor's face dropped, as if she had been cheated.

"What's this?" she said to Doreen accusingly. "He's perfectly able to do it."

"Of course he is," the girl replied. "He can do anything at all, when he wants to."

"Did you hear that?" the instructor called sneeringly to the others. "Let it be a lesson to you all. Riding is not a matter of letting the pony do what he likes, when he likes. It is a matter of making him do as he's told. Understood?"

The next exercise was to trot the ponies over a simple cross-pole. Again, no-one had any major problems, and Dominic was rewarded with a resounding "Well done!" Only Cuaifeach couldn't be bothered to jump such a paltry fence, but demolished it by trotting right through. The instructor didn't find it worthy of any comment, she just picked up the poles and fixed them at a height of about three feet. She knew this was really too high, too soon, but she wanted to see some action.

Rosie was the first to bungle her jump and a couple of the other ponies shied or tried to run out. Quite a few knocked the pole—it really was fixed too high. However, the main thing was to get each one to have a go, and this was attained with sound instructions and a little persuasion by the lunge-whip. In the end only Cuaifeach remained. As before, he was the last to go.

At first he wouldn't go anywhere near the fence but pranced around doing pirouettes like a ballerina. The instructor had to position herself behind him and crack the whip before he agreed to approach it in a disunited canter.

"Keep a tight hold on the reins!" she roared at Doreen's back. "Don't you dare let him get out of it!"

Doreen's knuckles went white on the reins as they approached the fence. But instead of jumping it, Cuaifeach put in a nasty sudden stop, enough to unseat his rider. She fell right on top of the fence, hitting her foot hard on one of the bars. The stallion rewarded himself with an invigorating exercise run around the school, until the instructor caught hold of his rein and gave a hard tug at his mouth to stop him.

"Get right back on," she ordered Doreen. "You have to show him that this kind of behaviour is not tolerated. He will jump that fence whether he likes it or not."

"I can't," the girl protested. "I've sprained my ankle."

"Well in that case," growled the instructor, not showing much concern, "I'm going to teach this spoilt pony a lesson. I'll show you all what riding is about."

Grabbing the top part of the lunge-whip, she jumped on his back. Cuaifeach winced a little, and Doreen looked on in alarm. The instructor dug her heels in to get him to go forward, but the pony did not move; he stood as if rooted to the ground. She hit him hard, first on one side, then the other. The stallion tried to buck, but found it hard with so much weight on his back, much more than he was used to. She hit him again and kicked him for all she was worth, thinking, I'll be damned if I'm going to let this pony make a fool of me in front of a class of pupils! To her relief, the desired effect was achieved. Cuaifeach sprang forward into a good active canter. She steered him sternly towards the jump and he cleared it with at least a foot to spare.

Triumphantly, she turned back to see the reaction of the class. That was all Cuaifeach needed to take over the reins as it were. He set off at a gallop and, taken off guard, all his rider could do to was cling to the saddle in a desperate attempt to stay on.

The stallion headed straight for the gate, a solid timber affair over four feet high. He jumped it without the slightest difficulty. The last the class saw of their instructor was her broad backside as it disappeared around the corner of the stable block.

"Gee whiz," said Dominic O'Neill. "Can that pony jump!"

4

New Year's Eve is often the saddest day of the year to people who are on their own, especially those who are not alone by choice. Even Christmas is not so bad, because at Christmas-time other people are more inclined to take mercy on you. This year, Julia had been invited by Doreen's mother and father to spend Christmas Day at their house. With the old granny and several of Doreen's brothers and sisters back from abroad, the Joyce family had thrown themselves headlong into the celebrations. They'd had their share of difficulties in years past, but all that was over, and now everyone brought their share of good food and laughter, presents and fun. Their home had been so full of seasonal warmth and joy that Julia hadn't felt she was missing anything.

But New Year was a different matter. She was bracing herself against the prospect of spending a long lonely evening accompanied only by the depressing memories of bygone, happier days.

It was therefore with genuine pleasure, greater

than she would have felt at any other time, that she received Wilfrid's call a few days after Christmas. He, too, seemed to be at a loose end. He was proposing to come down to Connemara for the New Year celebrations. He'd book into some nice hotel, he said, but only if she accepted his invitation to spend New Year's Eve with him. Julia did not need much persuasion.

She was even more pleased when he rang back to tell her that he'd got a reservation at Ballinahinch Castle. The hotel had been fully booked, but there had been a last-minute cancellation. Ballinahinch was one of Julia's favourite places: an old castle situated at the foot of a big mountain, overlooking a river and surrounded by woodland. Having been a private home for centuries, it still retained the comfortable atmosphere of a large country house.

As agreed, she met up with Wilfrid at lunchtime on New Year's Eve. After a snack lunch in the bar at Ballinahinch, they went for a long walk along the river. It was one of those days that occur now and then in midwinter in Connemara, when it's hard to believe that you've got your dates right: the sun was shining from a cloudless sky as warm as on a summer's day, birds were singing in the bushes and there was a lovely smell of moist earth, as if spring was only around the corner. In amongst the trees of the forest the first snowdrops had already appeared.

"Do you know anything about the history of this place?"Wilfrid asked Julia.

She was well able to fill him in. There had been a

castle at Ballinahinch for hundreds of years. It had been the seat of the Martyn family, who had owned most of the land in Connemara. Some of the Martyns had been colourful characters; stories about them still abounded. In Famine times they hadn't had the heart to collect rents from their poverty-stricken tenants and, as a result, the family had gone bankrupt, losing all they had, including the castle. In the early part of this century a sporting Indian maharajah had bought the place, settled there with his elephants and Rolls-Royces and spent his days fishing for salmon in the river. After he died, the castle had become a hotel. Parts of it still remained very much as he'd left it.

Wilfrid had to stop to take off his heavy winter coat. Little beads of perspiration were appearing above his eyebrows. Ballinahinch Lake lay glittering and blue before them under the jagged peak of Ben Lettery. Julia pointed out the little island with a small castle ruin. It had been used by Dick Martyn, nick-named Humanity Dick, Member of Parliament for Galway and founder of the RSPCA, to imprison people for the ill-treatment of animals. They were left there on bread and water until they promised to be kinder to their fellow creatures.

"And in the east we tend to look upon this part of Ireland as being uncivilised," said Wilfrid. "You learn something new every day."

On their return to the hotel they had tea in front of a roaring log fire, and then Wilfrid settled in the bar with the day's copy of *The Irish Times*, while Julia went to his room to change for dinner. She looked around at the luxurious furnishings and the panoramic view over the river and thought to herself that life wasn't without compensations.

The sequinned black evening dress hadn't been worn for years, but it still fitted. She took her time doing her hair and applying make up. Then, ready to go, she looked at the unfamiliar apparition in the tall mahogany mirror and said with some surprise, "I'd forgotten all about you."

Wilfrid's face bore an expression of unmitigated delight when he led her in to the cocktail reception. The hotel was beautifully decorated with old-fashioned tartan trimmings and a huge Christmas tree. They exchanged a few words with some of the other guests who, understandably, took them to be a married couple. Wilfrid certainly did little to suggest otherwise. Julia for her part fended off a slight feeling of claustrophobia stirring inside her, as if a trap was slowly closing around her.

The gala dinner had no less than seven courses: there was game pâté, mushroom soup, lemon sorbet, salmon soufflé, roast lamb, Grand Marnier parfait and a cheese board. As coffee was served, a jazz band played up, and it was announced that dancing was about to begin in the hall.

"I didn't know about the dancing," Wilfrid groaned. "I've eaten so much, I couldn't lift a finger!"

He was a man who took his digestion seriously.

Just as well, Julia thought. She thoroughly enjoyed the company of her old friend, but she didn't feel ready to go into a clinch with him.

At the stroke of twelve, champagne glasses were raised, there were cries of "Happy New Year!" loud cheers and the smacking sound of kisses all round. Wilfrid, after plucking up enough courage to give Julia a New Year kiss, was just about to apply it, when all the guests were asked to gather outside on the terrace. Julia was quick—quicker than she need have been, Wilfrid thought peevishly—to follow the instruction.

A splendid fireworks display lit up the sky and was reflected in the quiet dark waters of the Ballinahinch river. In the pitch black winter night the effect was spectacular. Wilfrid forgot his missed chance and put his arm protectively around Julia's shoulders.

Then he abandoned all fears of indigestion and pulled his partner onto the dance floor. He noted regrettably that, whilst excellent, the jazz was not of a type to invite any more intimate form of dancing. At least Julia seemed to be enjoying herself. In fact, she had suddenly remembered how much she loved dancing and how she had missed it in the past few years.

The party went on until the early hours of the morning.

When Julia finally drove back to Errislannan, she felt relaxed and happy. Being a widow at the age of thirty-two wasn't easy, and though she found it more bearable in Connemara than it had been in London, it still left a big gap in her life.

Whether Wilfrid was the right person to fill this vacuum was another matter. The main point in his favour was the fact that he was about the only contender. Even so, she didn't like to think of the look on his face when she wouldn't let him pull her close on the dance floor or when she had thanked him and said good-bye with only the chastest of pecks. To make up for her constraint, she had invited him for lunch the following day, and that had buoyed him up a bit. She just hoped that he wasn't going to expect more than lunch from her. She simply wasn't ready.

***

"Would you do me a favour?" Julia asked Wilfrid.

"Of course," he replied, smiling. They had finished lunch and were relaxing in armchairs in front of the fire in Julia's sitting-room. "Anything you say, my dear."

"Cuaifeach is due for a worm dose. I need someone to hold him for me."

Wilfrid's face took on the petulant look it always bore when he was displeased. How could she even ask such a thing, he thought to himself. He had already had one traumatic encounter with the stallion that day, when he arrived. Wise from experience, he had slipped through the gate very carefully without as much as touching the barrier, only to find his path barred by Cuaifeach's intimidating figure. He tried to duck to the left, then to the right, but the stallion moved quickly to ensure the visitor did not get anywhere near the house. In the end the beast had even pushed him backwards towards the gate, as if to show that the only way open to him was to go back to where he had come from.

Wilfrid had cowered by the gate feeling miserable. He could think of a thousand better ways of starting the New Year. His mother used to say that whatever happened to you on New Year's Day set the tone for the whole year ahead. That didn't augur well. The question was, what was he going to do? He couldn't very well call for Julia to come to his aid. It was quite bad enough being bullied by a ferocious stallion without having the lady of your choice witness your humiliation. Perhaps if he just stayed quiet, his antagonist would eventually get bored and turn his attentions elsewhere? As long as Julia didn't appear in the meantime.

Luck was definitely not on Wilfrid's side this New Year's Day. Julia had already been alerted to his dilemma and was walking towards him. He straightened up quickly and gave a nervous laugh, trying to look less like a frightened hare than he felt.

"Cuaifeach!" she called sternly. "Go to your stable!"

Amazingly, the animal immediately did exactly as he was told. Wilfrid looked on open-mouthed, as Julia shut the door on the pony.

"He understood what you said."

"Of course," she said lightly, bolting the door.

"How did you train him to do that?"

"Easy. He gets an apple each time he obeys. Only, now I have to get him one, to keep my end of the bargain."

Now Wilfrid, content and replete, couldn't think of anything he'd like to do less than help worm this beastly animal. The mere thought made his lunch lurch uneasily in his stomach.

"There's nothing to it," Julia assured him. "All you have to do is hold the rope while I insert the syringe."

At a loss for an honourable excuse, he shuffled out after her. Julia attached a lead-rope to Cuaifeach's head-collar and handed the end of it to Wilfrid. Then she squirted the worm paste deep into the pony's mouth and held his head high for a moment.

"I just want to make sure he doesn't spit it out," she explained. "I paid seven pounds for this paste. I wouldn't want to see it go to waste."

Cuaifeach, however, had not the slightest intention of swallowing the nasty paste. He gave a sudden jerk with his head and in one effective movement ejected the contents of his mouth. The blob of white worm paste landed on top of Wilfrid's head.

This time Julia couldn't help laughing. The sight of her companion with the large dollop on his head and a furious face to go with it could have reduced anyone to hysterics. "I'm sorry," she giggled. "Let's go in. I'll wash it out for you."

Wilfrid's good mood was gradually restored when

he had his scalp gently massaged with shampoo over the wash basin in Julia's bathroom. While he was still full of bitterness against the stallion who seemed committed to making a fool of him, he conceded that Julia couldn't be held responsible.

She offered him the use of her hair-dryer, but he said he'd rather let his hair dry in front of the fire. While Julia made some tea, he cleaned a few white splashes off his spectacles, and soon they were once more comfortably settled. Dusk was falling outside, and the room looked warm and cosy in the light of the fire. The only sound was the hissing of burning turf. Julia sat very still, and looking at her, Wilfrid felt a strange stirring in his chest. This time it was definitely not indigestion.

"To think," he said dreamily, "that we should have met again. Perhaps these things don't happen by chance...."

Julia made no reply. He put out his hand and placed it on top of hers.

"In all these years," he went on in a low voice, "I never stopped thinking about you...."

An almighty crash outside interrupted his train of thought. At least this time he did not have the teacup in his hand. Wilfrid jumped nevertheless, thinking to himself, why is it that these interruptions always came at the least suitable moment? Was the beast out there telepathic? Julia had got up and opened the window to look out. There was a sound of hoofbeat on gravel.

"He's kicked down the stable door," she stated in a

tired voice.

"I hope you're not going to ask me to go out and catch him!" was Wilfrid's immediate reaction.

"No," said Julia, watching Cuaifeach stop to take a deep draught from the rainwater barrel. "The barrier is in place, so he can stay out. I'll get someone to repair the door in the morning."

Wilfrid went up to join her. The air from the open window was sweet and mild, not at all what you'd expect in midwinter. The semi-darkness made Julia's face look gently alluring, veiled in its own mystery. He put his hands on her slim shoulders. "Julia," he whispered. "There was never anyone else for me. After you, how could there be?"

She was standing with her head bowed, her gaze fixed firmly on a spot on the carpet.

"Look at me," Wilfrid pleaded softly.

When she didn't, he leant forward until his head was level with hers. Because he was so much taller than her, it meant bending almost double. He stared at her intently, willing her to turn her face towards him. It's only a matter of seconds, he told himself, seconds before her lips will meet mine.... Julia stood impassive, her breath bated, thinking desperately, my God, what will happen now?

What did happen was that Wilfrid let off a resounding yell. He shot up, clutching the nape of his neck with both hands, and swivelled round to find himself face to face with Cuaifeach. The stallion had stopped to stick his head in through the open window. Water was still dripping from his mouth, which he was just after planting on the back of Wilfrid's neck.

"I have ice-cold water running down my spine!" Wilfrid complained. "He's doing it on purpose. This blasted animal is determined to get me out of here! Well I'm telling you, if you ever want to see me again, you'll have to get rid of him!"

Julia, secretly grateful for Cuaifeach's intervention, tried to explain: "He's not used to strange men coming here."

That, at least, was one piece of information that could only appease Wilfrid. He calmed down a little.

"Once he realises that you are a friend, that you have as much right as he to be here, he'll accept you."

Wilfrid frowned, trying to interpret exactly what her statement implied, as far as he was concerned.

"You go out and talk to him," she went on to say, "while I tidy up the kitchen. He'll understand every word you say. Give him a pat, make it clear to him that you want to be his friend. Tell him there is room enough for both of you."

She went out to the kitchen, leaving a rather pale-faced Wilfrid behind. He felt she might as well have asked him to stick his head into the mouth of a lion. At first he had no intention of following suit. But then he thought of Eric O'Reilly, Julia's late husband, whom she had obviously thought the world of. He had been famous for his way with horses; there wasn't a race horse in the world that hadn't done his best for him. It was inevitable that Julia would draw her own comparisons with every other man she met. In his case it would hardly be a favourable one if she discovered that he did not even have the courage to pat a Connemara pony.

He went out through the kitchen door just to get a chance to say, nonchalantly, "I'll do as you suggested. Have a word with the old boy out there." To himself he thought, I'm glad none of my colleagues in the office will be there to hear me actually *talking* to a horse!

Some thirty seconds later he reappeared at the kitchen door, clutching his left arm, his face contorted with pain. As Julia looked up, she thought he was about to faint.

"He bit me," Wilfrid moaned. "When I put out my hand to pat him. Oh God, I'm going to lose my arm.... And I'm not up to date on my tetanus injections!"

Julia sat him down on a chair and gently pulled off his jacket. Then she rolled up his shirt sleeve. On the forearm there was an imprint of strong stallion teeth, red and blue, already surrounded by considerable swelling. Fortunately the skin wasn't broken.

"It's not too bad, Wilfrid," she comforted him. "I'll give you some painkillers. At least it's your left arm, it won't affect your work."

Cuaifeach, drawn to the light of the open kitchen door, was peering in nosily, his brown eyes shining with a gleam of wicked delight.

"Go away!" Julia snapped at him. "This time you've really gone too far!"

Friends in Need

5

People are funny. They will fret endlessly over something, only to find out eventually that it wasn't worth worrying about in the first place, and in the same way, they don't worry half as much as they should about things that are really worth fretting over. When you think about it, the amount of worry we put in is never quite in proportion to the matter of concern. It makes you wonder, what's the point of worrying at all?

Doreen had been anxious for days about having to face Julia and when she saw the white car drive up outside her house she felt none of the usual pleasure at seeing her friend. Her leg in plaster had provided an excuse not to go over and see her, but now there was no escape. She'd have to tell her.

Julia, too, looked uneasy as she entered the kitchen. Perhaps she could sense something unpleasant in the air?

"Don't get up," she said, seeing Doreen reach for her crutch. "How is your ankle?"

It had turned out that Doreen's ankle was badly

broken, not just sprained, after her fall at the O'Briens.

"It's stopped hurting," Doreen replied, "but I'll be in plaster for a good while yet. God knows how long it will be before I can ride again."

"That's really too bad," Julia said thoughtfully, as if pondering the implications of this.

"Uncle Christy is so funny," Doreen went on, trying to defer the uncomfortable moment of telling Julia the truth. "He keeps going on at me, saying I must sue the O'Briens out of sight and collect a whole lot of money off the insurance that Roc O'Neill took out for them. He says he heard of a man got ten thousand for a broken ankle. I keep telling him, and so does my dad, that we wouldn't want to get involved in that kind of thing, but Uncle Christy just can't leave it alone. You know what he's like."

Julia did. Doreen's grand-uncle always had a bee in his bonnet about something. "On the other hand," she said, "you have a genuine case. You said yourself that the fence was set far too high. I'm sure there are many people in this country claiming damages who are less justified than yourself."

"But I knew what I was letting myself in for," Doreen retorted. "It's not as if anyone forced me to ride my own pony. You should hear mam on the subject...."

"Oh? What does she have to say?" Julia knew that Doreen's mother had always been unhappy about her daughter riding a stallion—and a difficult one at that.

Doreen pulled a face. "She says it's all Cuaifeach's fault, that it serves me right for getting on such a dangerous pony." Her face suddenly got very serious, and she was silent for a moment. Then, unable to contain it any longer, she blurted out: "Dominic wants to take Cuaifeach. Take him to Dublin to try him jumping."

She glanced at Julia to see how she would take it. All she noted was an expression of pure astonishment. Doreen looked down on her plaster cast. "I told him he could," she mumbled. "I thought it would be a good idea to get him away from here for a while, to give Mam a chance to settle down. I mean, it's not as if he's going to be any use to me anyhow for some time. Only I didn't think of you, Julia. Will you be awfully cross with me?"

"Cross?" Julia repeated. "Why should I be cross with you?"

"I don't want you to think I'm not grateful," Doreen began. "After you looked after him so well, not even charging me for it.... I promise, I would never have taken him away if it hadn't been for mam."

"Hang on!" Julia interrupted. "If I could get a word in edgeways, I'll tell you why I'm here."

Doreen looked up.

"I came to tell you that, quite apart from the fact that I've had just about as much as I can take of your delightful stallion, I won't have the time to look after him any more, because I'm starting a new project. But I felt terrible about telling you this when

I knew you're not in a state to look after him yourself."

"You don't mind?" Doreen said incredulously. "You don't mind Dominic taking him?"

Julia smiled. "I think it's a wonderful idea."

When Doreen's mother and father came in, they, too, were relieved to learn that everyone was in agreement. It took a great worry off their chest, Sean Joyce said.

"With some luck he'll go on to become a champion," he said as they were all seated in the kitchen with cups of steaming tea. "Then we can travel the country to applaud his victories, having none of the trouble of looking after him. Life will be easier for all of us."

"And safer for Doreen," her mother added.

Doreen said nothing. As far as she was concerned, the arrangement with Dominic was only temporary.

Far away they heard the muffled noise of an engine, punctuated with frequent cracks and bangs. It seemed to be coming their way.

"That sounds like Christy," Sean Joyce deduced. "No-one else has an exhaust like that. How he keeps it from falling to pieces I don't know."

It was indeed Doreen's grand-uncle in his ramshackle car. He jumped out, showing signs of great excitement. He didn't even stop to close the car door behind him, but rushed straight into the Joyces' kitchen brandishing a copy of the *Connacht Tribune*.

"Have ye seen what's on the paper?" he cried.

The newspaper was placed on the kitchen table,

crumples smoothed out so that everyone could read the advertisement on the back page:

CALLING ALL OWNERS OF CONNEMARA PONIES
FRIENDS OF THE CONNEMARA PONY
INVITE YOU TO A WINTER SOCIAL AT THE CLIFDEN
VIEW HOTEL
SATURDAY, JANUARY 27TH AT 9 PM
A FREE DRINK FOR EACH PONY—BRING REGISTRATION
DOCUMENTS!

"A free drink for each pony!" Christy called out, ramming his index finger up and down the last two lines of the ad. "Isn't it a shame I've only got the one mare!"

"Who are these 'Friends of the Connemara Pony?'" Julia wanted to know.

"I haven't a clue. No-one ever heard of them. Not that anyone will mind, as long as they give out free drink."

"Do you think a lot of pony owners will show up?" Julia asked.

Christy gave her a look as if her question was more than tolerably naive. "Everyone will be there!" he said. "There's not a man in Connemara would miss a chance like that. You'd better get yourself a pony, Sean, or they won't let you in."

"I wonder," Julia said reflectively, "if this is not the kind of opportunity I've been hoping for."

And then she told them about her project.

She had been working on it since November, ever

since the day when she first met Wilfrid again. To begin with, she had merely done what he had recommended, got in touch with a number of people she knew in England who might help her find a buyer for her colt foals. But one thing led to another, and in due course she had been given an introduction to a riding club in the South-East. They specialised in breaking and training young horses and ponies. Some were kept for the members and their children, others were sold on in due course. With several hundred members, they were always on the lookout for high quality mounts, especially Connemaras, whose sound conformation, high intelligence and good natural paces made them ideal performance ponies. Basically, what they had said in a recent letter to Julia was that they would be prepared to buy as many as thirty young ponies from Connemara, provided she could assist them with the selection and negotiate prices no higher than the going English market rates, allowing for the cost of transport and VAT. And what was more, if this first batch was successful, they had every intention of coming back for more.

Christy was struggling to take in the enormity of all this. His eyebrows were knit together so tightly, they almost met above his nose.

"It means that local breeders will be selling directly to the market," Julia explained. "There'll be no dealers, no middlemen."

"Except you'll want your cut," Christy filled in. "Not that that's anything but fair," he added quickly, so as not to offend her.

"I will certainly not take a cut," Julia declared firmly. "It's time pony owners in Connemara got to see for themselves what their ponies are really worth."

The only question was how best to spread the news. She had thought of advertising, but this Winter Social seemed to be a better way of informing people about her intentions.

The two men appeared strangely hesitant.

"Is there any reason why I shouldn't?" she asked them.

"Well I don't know," said Sean, forthright as ever. "It's not usual in these parts to go public on such matters."

"Why ever not?"

"Oh you know," he expounded. "It's always better to be discreet, like. Once word gets out that you're after ponies, people start putting up their prices. You won't get such a good deal."

"But that's exactly what I want," Julia replied.

The men, Doreen and her mother all looked at her perplexed.

"The whole idea is to pay them well, encourage them to hold on to their good breeding-stock and produce more ponies."

They still seemed confused, so she told them what Wilfrid had revealed about the crisis facing the Connemara pony, the real risk the region ran of losing its ponies forever.

"I don't believe we have time to wait for the

Department to act," she concluded. "What I propose to do will be more effective, and I'm going to do it right now."

Nobody spoke for a while. Doreen stared listlessly, as she often did these days, out of the window at the bleak January day, while her mother washed up and her father tended the fire. Christy for his part was thinking hard, sucking his few remaining teeth.

"It's no job for a lady like yourself," he said eventually. "No-one would want to be dealing with a woman, sure."

"They'll all want to deal with me," said Julia, "when they see that I pay over the odds."

Christy's wrinkled face suddenly became animated. "Why don't you just leave the whole thing to me!" he suggested. "I'll put a nice deal together for you. The usual way. Don't worry, I'll see you get exactly what you want."

Julia smiled. She knew Christy only too well. "And you'll get what you want," she said. "Your cut. That's what you have in mind, isn't it?"

Christy looked embarrassed. Sean winked at her behind his back. Doreen and her mother looked away, as if they wanted to have no part of this conversation. Julia got up.

"Thank you for offering," she said, "but I've made up my mind. I know exactly what I'm doing."

"It sounds like a lot of hard work for nothing," Sean Joyce mumbled.

"Not for nothing," Julia corrected him. She did not elaborate further. They wouldn't understand; no-one could possibly understand the feeling that had plagued her ever since Eric died. With his demanding career as a top jockey, her adult life had been spent in support of him. Losing him had left her with an awful feeling of belonging nowhere, of being no good to anyone. Now she was hoping that, by doing something useful for her adopted community, she might be able to fill the terrible void inside her. To be needed and appreciated once more, to feel that her contribution mattered.... That was all she wished for. And if all it took to achieve it was some hard work, that was a price she was more than willing to pay.

***

The following Saturday night, the lobby of the Clifden View Hotel was packed with pony owners queuing up to be admitted into the conference room set aside for the social. A table had been placed close by the entrance and a smooth-haired man in a navy blazer was checking the registration papers, noting down the name of each owner and pony before handing out drink tokens and letting people in.

"What do you want with the names?" one man asked suspiciously. "Surely you won't be sending us all Christmas cards?"

The man in the navy blazer looked taken aback for a moment, but then he smiled disarmingly.

"To avoid duplications," was his glib reply. "We can't have people going out and coming in again, taking undue advantage of our offer. We have to keep some sort of check."

"That's a sensible precaution," Sean Joyce commented, handing in Cuaifeach's papers, lent to him for the night by his daughter. "God knows there's nothing on earth so wily as a man after free drink."

Further back in the queue, Julia discovered a few familiar faces. There was Bertie Nee, the bachelor from Streamstown who kept urging her to come out for a drink, though she never accepted, and right next to her was the Cashel crowd, headed by Marty MacDonagh, Cuaifeach's breeder. As always, he was anxious for news of his protégé, and she told him about the stallion's latest depredations. The men howled with laughter, Marty most of all, his pleasure heightened by relief that these matters were no longer his concern.

"Still going around like the *cuaifeach*," he chuckled, referring to the wicked whirlwind that had given the pony his name. "I'm glad to hear he hasn't changed."

The queue moved steadily forward, as each man and the odd woman produced their certificates and collected their tokens. Most of them kept only one or possibly two ponies; it's rare in Connemara to find people with land that can support a larger number. But suddenly the queue came to a halt. There appeared to be some dispute at the door.

Joe Will and Tom Samuel, two cousins, rough customers who lived way up in the wilderness of the

Bens, had handed in a whole stack of documents, soiled and tattered but nevertheless valid, according to themselves. They now demanded thirty-seven free drinks in return.

The man in the navy blazer thumbed through the papers, a look of consternation on his face. "Some of these are over thirty years old!" he exclaimed.

"So?" said Tom Samuel, blowing a cloud of smoke from his cigarette in his face.

"Most of these ponies must be long dead and gone."

"They were all alive this morning," Joe Will assured him. "Alive and kicking, so they were."

"That's right," Tom Samuel affirmed. "One of them kicked me in the butt."

The man in the blazer pursed his lips. "I would need to see some proof of that."

"Proof?" said Tom Samuel. "It said naught about proof on the paper. But if you insist, I can always show it to you.... A mighty bruise," he said, indicating his rear end.

The man looked horrified, but there was much amusement among the people thronging around them.

"What'd you expect us to do?" Joe Will demanded in his loud aggressive voice. "Bring them along? All thirty-seven? It's a tight enough squeeze as it is."

Everyone was laughing now. The man in the navy blazer reflected that, but for some quick thinking on his part, these louts would soon get the better of him. "There will be no tokens issued for ponies over the age of twenty," he declared.

"What?" Christy squeaked. "That will rule out my Molly! Come on, this is cheating. I'm going to complain! Where is the boss?"

Furious, he pushed his way through the crowd, past Joe Will and Tom Samuel, until he was facing the man at the table.

"I want to see the boss!" he announced. "Where is he?"

"Er...he's not here." The man in the navy blazer was beginning to look seriously harassed.

"Well who is he? I want to have a word with him. He owes me a drink. I haven't come all this way just to be fobbed off with a sudden new ruling like that."

"Listen," the man said placatingly to Joe Will and Tom Samuel. "Here are twenty drink tokens. It's more than you should have, you know that as well as I do."

Joe Will and Tom Samuel looked at each other, then shrugged and took the proffered tokens. After all, it wasn't every day that someone stood them twenty free drinks. And as Christy vociferously maintained that his Molly was every bit as good as any other pony, he too was given his token without even having to mention his name or show his papers. Anything to get rid of a trouble-maker, the blazer man seemed to think.

However, that wasn't the end of his problems. In front of Julia in the queue was a person carrying a large cardboard box. She had noticed him as they both entered, a rather distinguished-looking man, tall and slim with curly blond hair, dressed in a smart sports jacket and an expensive pair of shoes, such as you rarely saw on the feet of a Connemara man. He had nodded and greeted most of the others, but did not chat with any of them, just waited patiently for his turn. The to-do at the door he had watched with measured interest. When he arrived at the table, he plonked down the heavy cardboard box in front of the man in the navy blazer, meeting his eye with just the slightest hint of provocation.

"What's this?" the man asked guardedly, his voice slightly shriller than before.

"It contains the current passports for my Connemaras," the other man replied politely. "One hundred and sixty-four of them. All, I guarantee, in a perfect state of health. Perhaps you'd like to count them yourself, to make sure?" he suggested amiably.

The man in the navy blazer looked at him aghast. "Sh...sh...surely you don't mean...." he stuttered.

"I do," said the man, smiling. "It is my full intention to collect a token for each one of them."

"That's not possible," came a feeble protest. "What will they say... I mean, just consider the cost of it...."

"You tell your superiors that if they make offers like this, they had better stand by them. If they renege, I shall certainly make them answer for it."

The man in the navy blazer realised that he was on boggy ground, but like many people in such a position he decided to respond by launching a counterattack. "Little did I think," he said maliciously, in a loud voice so that everyone would hear, "that you of all people were so desperate for drink."

The other man was unruffled. "Everyone knows I don't touch the stuff. I'll have no part of your rotten party either. I just thought I'd share my tokens out amongst the crowd. But never you mind," he continued serenely, picking up his box again. "I really just wanted to show what I think of your methods. I'm surprised at you, Michael Sullivan, for letting yourself be dragged into something of this order. All I can say is, I hope they pay you well for it."

And with that he departed.

The man called Michael Sullivan did his best to appear unconcerned, but Julia noticed that his ears had turned an interesting shade of dark red.

Once admitted, she lost no time seeking out Johnny Tass to find out more about all this. Johnny, of course, was the best informed person in Connemara. People used to say he knew about things before they happened. His nickname he didn't owe for nothing to the Russian news agency. The man with the box, he informed Julia, was Bill Ryan, field-master of the Galway Blazers, the famous County Galway hunt, and he had the largest herd of Connemaras in the country. Johnny summed him up as a good, able man.

That was probably a fair assessment, Julia mused. Public opinion, for which Johnny Tass was the self-proclaimed spokesman, seldom went wrong in matters of character reference. In a closed community such as this, a good name had to be earned and, likewise, it was easily lost.

But when she asked Johnny about Michael Sullivan, he was strangely reticent. "A yes-man," was all she got out of him. "From Galway." As for the incident at the door, he was equally unhelpful. He had already been inside when it took place and so, to his chagrin, had missed it.

With all the guests admitted to the conference room and provided with their first round of drinks, Michael Sullivan took to the podium at the end of the room and called for silence. He cleared his throat whilst waiting for the din to die down, reminding himself that this was his moment. He took great pride in his ability to speak in public and was in no doubt that this special talent was the main reason why he had been selected to act as front man to the group.

The crowd were gazing up at him. Being of short stature himself, he savoured the unusual experience of looking down at others. Smiling, he started the well-rehearsed speech with which he had been issued:

"Dear friends," he began in the intimate, confidential tone that never failed to hook the listeners. "On behalf of the Friends of the Connemara Pony, I would like to wish you all welcome to this Winter Social. It is indeed an honour to see so many of you gathered here tonight. All the Friends will be delighted."

"Who are these friends of yours?" called a voice in the crowd. "We like to know who we're dealing with."

"Oh, you know them all," Michael Sullivan said dismissively, trying not to show his irritation at having his beautiful speech interrupted. "I won't mention any names, in case I pass someone over. But like yourselves, we all consider ourselves the true friends of the Connemara Pony, a beautiful animal, unique in the world."

He paused to check whether his reply would be accepted. Relieved that there were no more awkward interruptions, he continued in his deep, resonant voice that some people found surprising coming from such a slight man. "The purpose of tonight's gathering is to congratulate you all on the wonderful work you have done and are continually doing on behalf of this marvellous breed. It is a contribution you can be justly proud of. As we all know, it stretches back over decades, even centuries, and in all these years, no hardship, no privations, have ever stopped the people of Connemara providing the world with his very best product: the Connemara pony. We want you all to know that your efforts are being duly appreciated. We recognise the fact that you have created something that has a value far beyond money. You have enriched the world by giving it an equine species that cannot be equalled. And the world depends on you, Connemara breeders, to continue the good work. Even in the face of hard times and recession, we all look to you to keep the best of the breed going. Not necessarily for commercial rewards, but for the pride and prestige that comes of producing the best. I would like to propose a toast to you all. To you, Connemara breeders, and to our beloved Connemara pony. *Slainté!*"

Glasses were raised and hands were clapped, though not very effectively, since everyone was balancing a full glass. Julia tried to work out what exactly the man up there was aiming at. It would be nice if she could somehow link her address on to his. After all, they seemed to share a common objective: to encourage breeders to produce more ponies, even though he seemed to think it could be done with pretty words rather than tangible benefits. However, there was no time to reflect on these differences. If she wanted to make her voice heard in this crowd, she'd better do so at once, before the free drinks began to take effect.

Though Michael Sullivan seemed to have finished his speech, he still lingered on the podium, reluctant, as it were, to step down. Julia went up and told him that she would like to add a few words.

The man looked at her in alarm. "I don't think we can allow that," he said.

"Since when did you need permission to open your mouth in this country?" an old man standing next to her called out. He was Ger Folan, one of the mainstays of the Connemara Pony Society and highly respected everywhere. His intervention made Michael Sullivan hesitate for a moment.

"You get up there, girl, and say what you have to say," Ger Folan directed her. "I'm sure we're all interested."

Michael Sullivan glared at her as she took up her place on the podium. He didn't step aside but stayed centre stage as if he wanted to show them all that he was still in charge.

Sensing his hostility, which he did not do much to conceal, Julia decided first of all to explain the background to her project. Since everyone present had a vested interest in the continued welfare of the Connemara Pony breed, this was bound to make sense to them all, even to Michael Sullivan.

"I'm sure you know," she began, "that good ponies are becoming scarce on the ground in Connemara. Many of you here tonight will have sold off ponies in recent months...."

She could see men on the floor nodding their heads in agreement and looking up expectantly to hear more. Only Michael Sullivan's face expressed scepticism.

"Official statistics show a rapid decline in the number of Connemara-based ponies," she continued, anxious to show him that she had done her homework. "I have been informed by the Department of Agriculture that unless something is done to reverse this trend, Connemara runs a risk of losing its ponies altogether."

Before she even got to the end of her sentence, she realised she'd made a mistake. The mere mention of official statistics and the Department had caused misgivings to be written all over people's faces. It was as if an invisible curtain had been drawn between her and the floor. Michael Sullivan was not late to take advantage.

"This is all alarmist government propaganda," he said scornfully. "Surely we haven't got together to listen to such nonsense."

"You be quiet, Michael Sullivan," Ger Folan ordered him. "We heard you out, and this young lady is entitled to the same courtesy."

Quickly realising she would soon lose the ear of everybody, Julia changed tack. She told them briefly that she was looking for some thirty good quality ponies, up to the age of four. English market prices, less the cost of transport and VAT, would be paid for them, and that, she promised, would be a good sight more than they were used to getting. There'd be no cuts, no commission payable at either end. Anyone with a suitable pony for sale was welcome to contact her.

Michael Sullivan was staring at her blankly. His ears had gone a deep purple. In a sudden movement, he pushed past her, holding out his arm as if he wanted to sweep her off the podium, she actually had to take a step backwards to avoid being swiped in the face.

"Now this is exactly the sort of thing we want to stop," he said. "Foreigners coming in to exploit the local breeders, taking the good stock away, robbing you of your most valuable asset. Believe me," he added in a low confidential voice, "the development of the Connemara pony owes nothing to greed. Oh, no. It owes everything—everything—to people like yourselves and your forebears. People who put honour before paltry profits. People to whom a red rosette in Clifden means more than all the money in the world."

He looked smugly at the crowd as if expecting an applause, but their only reaction was one of extreme wariness, the exact opposite to what he had hoped for. Julia, for her part, was equally disappointed with the response to her proposal.

"Do you have any questions?" she asked, to encourage them to air any doubts they might have.

One big strong man put his hand up. "Why are you doing this?" he wanted to know. "What's in it for you?"

Julia was prepared for that question.

"The same that's in it for everyone else," she replied. "With some luck I'll get to sell my own colt foals. I can assure you I intend to put them forward, though the final decision will of course rest with the buyer."

Another man was elbowing his way up to the front. Much to her dismay, Julia recognised her hostile neighbour, Jim Lydon, a person whose presence she could well have done without at this juncture. Her previous contacts with this man had left her in no doubt that he hardly admired her. Johnny Tass had made light of the fact, told her it was nothing personal. Jim was simply one of these people who go through life pretending to be superior to everyone else. It's the easiest trick in the world, he said. All you have to do is find fault with everyone else, refuse to see anything worthy in them whilst ignoring your own shortcomings. The world is full of Jim Lydons and they're all miserable, he ended with a wink.

Be that as it may. It didn't help her here and now. Besides, Jim Lydon, though liked by few, was respected by many. You could tell by the attention they showed when he turned to face the crowd, as if they expected something worthwhile to come out of him.

"I don't know what this woman will have ye believe," he announced, his features arranged in their usual snide look. "The whole thing is ridiculous. Why would these English people buy our ponies at the going market rate? If they were going to pay the same price, they might as well buy their ponies in England."

Michael Sullivan nodded ostentatiously in agreement.

"They happen to think," Julia said in a voice trembling with suppressed anger, "that the ponies coming out of Connemara are of better quality than those bred overseas. Even if the price is the same, they'll get better value for their money buying them here. Is there anyone present tonight," she addressed the floor, "who is going to argue that point with me?"

There wasn't. Unable to think of a suitable retort, Jim Lydon just shook his head and snorted as he always did when at a loss for words. Michael Sullivan, on the other hand, had a sudden inspiration.

"It's all money," he called out in a shrill voice. "She'll be turning your heads with her talk of money. All I can say is," he concluded, lowering his voice so that he sounded rather like a priest in his pulpit, "that a wise man is he who resists the call of the purse."

After that he looked back at Julia. So there, he seemed to say. She half expected him to cock her a snook as well. Then he stepped down from the podium, and the crowd, relieved to see formalities at an end, started chatting amongst themselves. It annoyed Julia that he should have walked off with the last word, but there was nothing she could do about it. She was even more upset to find, when she stepped down, that people, even those she knew, were turning away from her. The only one who would talk to her was Ger Folan.

"Good girl," he said with a wink from his watery blue old man's eyes. "You give them folks what they deserve."

Julia was getting more and more confused.

"I'll tell you one thing," Ger went on. "You're the most courageous woman I have ever come across. In a long and eventful life. That's quite something."

"Courageous?" Julia repeated. "What on earth have I done that's courageous? I'm just trying to be helpful, in a way that makes perfect sense to me."

Ger gave her a look containing so much sympathy it bordered on pity. "I don't suppose you know," he said, "how things go in Connemara."

"What do you mean, Ger? Please tell me."

He shrugged good-humouredly. "You get on with

your project, by all means. But don't let it worry you too much if it falls flat on its face."

"Why should it?" Julia wanted to know. "It's going to benefit a lot of people. Why shouldn't it succeed?"

Ger just smiled again, his kindly old man's smile. "You don't know how things go in Connemara," he repeated.

Julia went home soon after. It wasn't much fun to be at a party where people seemed afraid of talking to her, or possibly of being seen talking to her. She was determined to find out why this should be so, but realised that this night was not the right occasion to pursue the issue.

On her way to the car she heard hurried footsteps behind her. It was a man called Patsy Lynch, a friend of Johnny Tass. "Hey, Julia," he said in a hushed voice, beckoning to her to join him in a dark nook just off Main Street. "I have a nice filly," he told her, still in the same husky voice. "Three-year-old, good bone, nearly fourteen hands. I'd say she'd do for you."

"That's great," Julia said, pleased to have at least one person taking her up on her offer. "I'll come over and see her tomorrow afternoon, if that suits you."

"You have a deal," he hissed, brushing against her. She had a fleeting impression of his hand groping inside her coat pocket, but thought no more of it until she came home and fumbled in the same pocket for her house key. Then she found it. A twenty pound note. She stared at it in amazement. Ger is right, she thought. I have no idea how things go in Connemara.

6

The day was mild and soft with little wind—nothing to complain about, except that now, towards the end of the afternoon, the warm-up area located out-of-doors had turned into a sea of mud. Dominic winced as he cantered around the edge and his brilliant white breeches filled with grey smudges. By the time he entered the arena, his legs would look like the snow leopard in Dublin Zoo.

There were two practice jumps, one upright and one spread, and after warming up he popped Cuaifeach over the two of them in rapid succession. The stallion jumped with about as much effort as if they had been poles on the ground. Dominic was aware of people watching and pointing as he trotted down towards the gate.

Cuaifeach was indeed a sight for sore eyes. He had been clipped all over, a procedure he had never been subjected to in Connemara and hadn't much relished, but it certainly showed off the powerful muscles under his skin. Weeks of huge rations of concentrated nutrition had also taken effect. He had put on over a hundred pounds, but with the hard work he was doing, none of it had gone to fat, only active working condition. The infusions of extra vitamins and minerals had made his coat so glossy you could see your reflection in it. His eyes were deep and clear like springs in the forest—a sure sign of health and well-being.

Added to this was Dominic's turnout, faultless as ever, that is until the moment he entered the warm-up area. Now Cuaifeach's legs were spattered with mud like his own, but there wasn't much they could do about that. At least his tack was shining and his mane was neatly done up in plaits. The latter had taken most of the morning to achieve, because of Doreen's instructions that not a hair was to be pulled from his thick bushy mane. The plaits therefore were about four times longer and more numerous than need be, and took at least four times longer to do. Dominic was becoming a wizard with needle and thread.

He needn't really have concerned himself with the grooming of the pony, since all such services were supplied—at a price—by the livery stable where he was kept. But Dominic knew that looking after a pony was just as important as riding him if you aspired towards a close working partnership. He enjoyed fussing over the stallion, and Cuaifeach took an obvious delight in his attentions. There was no doubt that the lengthy grooming sessions before each competition had helped cement their friendship.

Where work was concerned, things were going very well, or as well as could be expected, according to Brian, Dominic's highly qualified private instructor. Initially, Brian had been sceptical about taking on a wild pony from Connemara that had never jumped a fence apart from that surrounding his own paddock. But he only had to see Cuaifeach once, see his beautiful arched outline over the jumps and his perfect natural balance, to realise that he had a remarkable talent on his hands. The stallion had a vigorous high jump in him just waiting to come out, and he approached the fences with care and confidence. The only thing lacking in him was impulsion. It seemed impossible to get him to jump more than two fences in sequence.

Brian applied every method and trick that he could think of to get the stallion to complete a course. He got on him himself, used the best of his skills, put his spurs on and cajoled, commanded and threatened in turn. To get a horse to perform, he explained to Dominic, you have to find the key to unlock him. That sounded awfully professional, except for the fact that Cuaifeach seemed to be a complete deadlock. He never got past fence number three, and even that was a concession, from the stallion's point of view. In Connemara he had never bothered to jump more than one fence at a time.

In the end the trainer had to abandon all his high-flying principles and resort to a low form of bribery. A bucket of nuts was rattled behind each fence as the stallion approached it. It worked wonders, Cuaifeach jumped eight fences in a row. After that he was given the bucket as a reward.

"It is important to condition him into thinking of completing the course as a means to a tasty end," Brian explained. "Now we know the key to his heart. It goes through his stomach."

Dominic, however, remembered something Doreen had said when she handed him over. "You'll find that he bargains with you. He won't do anything for nothing. He just can't see why he should."

Halting by the board at the entrance to the indoor school, Dominic checked his place and was pleased to see that he was fourth. It paid off being early at these competitions where you jumped in the order you entered. Waiting around for ages watching others perform was no good, it made both him and Cuaifeach edgy, so that by the time it was their turn they had lost that state of poised alertness that Brian said you needed to jump well. Dominic could feel it now, like a tight knot in his stomach; competition nerves, nothing to fear or fight, just raw energy coiled up, waiting to be released. Vibrations of something similar emanated from the massive body underneath him. It was amazing, Dominic thought, how after only a few weeks they already shared so much.

He entered the pocket. The course builder was just checking the last of the fences and before long it was announced that the course was open to inspection. It didn't look too bad, Dominic reflected, a couple of uprights, a few spreads, a double combination and one final triple. That was the one to watch. Cuaifeach hadn't jumped many of those. Otherwise the course was all right. The stallion seemed to think so too. He sniffed at one or two of the fences and gazed benignly at the others, as if they were good friends just waiting to be cleared by him.

We're going to make it! Dominic said to himself with a pang of excitement. We'll show them all, won't we, Cuaifeach? It occurred to him that he really wanted to show them all very badly. Brian, for one. He couldn't get over what Brian had said, that, given his natural ability, Cuaifeach could go all the way to the top. "Could," he had said, not *"will"* or even *"should"*. It was as if he held something back, some secret proviso, a qualifying clause beginning with "if" or even "if only". Well, today Dominic intended to show him that he could stuff his damned proviso.

Doreen was another person he dearly wanted to show, if for entirely different reasons. "He really is a very good pony," she had told him. "It's just that he doesn't know it himself." That was another point. Wouldn't it be great to show Cuaifeach himself exactly what he was capable of?

To spare himself at this sensitive moment, Dominic deliberately passed over the person he wanted most of all to show what he and Cuaifeach were worth together—his father Roc—who had no faith whatsoever in his son's ability, who had said he wouldn't buy him a jumping pony unless he first proved himself, sounding as if he never expected this to happen. His reaction when he heard that Dominic was taking on Cuaifeach had been,"That crackpot pony? Oh well, I suppose he'll do for you."

As a matter of fact, Dominic wasn't by nature wildly competitive. Unlike his father, he derived little pleasure from beating opponents. However, one instinct he seemed to have inherited from the Olympic gold medallist: an urge to do well. In this he was encouraged by his mother, who was a born perfectionist, the type of woman who never has a hair out of place, who gets up an hour before the rest of the family to make herself presentable before breakfast. Dominic's mother had always impressed upon her son the need to look and act your best, in that order, as if the one depended on the other. In her view it did. She maintained quite seriously that a flawless appearance was the first step towards success in life.

In Dominic's case, however, the immaculate turnout was more a reflection of his own level of commitment. He was haunted by his desire to do well, even excel. So far this desire had remained unfulfilled, for the simple reason that there was nothing that he did particularly well, except dress, but that was all thanks to his mother, who spent most of her days browsing in shops at the expense of her estranged wealthy husband. His school results were mediocre, he was only reasonably good at games and, in spite of endless coaching from his ambitious dad, had never attained more than average swimming standards. The only sweet success he had ever tasted had been in the show ring with Rosie, and even that limited victory had owed more to looks and impressions than actual skill. Show-jumping was different; here ability, judgement, rhythm and balance all came together in a pursuit of true excellence. What was more, when you got it right, you knew it, and so did everyone else. There could be no doubting or arguing about it. No-one could ever take it away from you.

There was still an awful long way to go, a lot of hard work, followed by even more hard work, but Dominic was prepared for that. His first goal had been set: to have Cuaifeach graded for "C" competitions before the end of the season. For that he would need fifty points. Two points were awarded for each double clear round. It didn't seem much for such a big effort, but Brian had explained the thinking behind it: to stop people overjumping their novice mounts, forcing them against the clock before they were ready for it. In "D" competitions like the one he was about to enter, there was no clock, no internal competition. All that was required for the measly two points was two successive clear rounds. If he got his first double clear today, as he was confident he would, he'd only have another twenty-four to go.

The bell went for the first rider, a blonde girl on a pretty chestnut mare. He had seen them before, they went to all the competitions. The girl rode well and her pony was very keen though rather careless; she rushed her fences and rarely made it around the course without knocking a pole or two. Today she was worse than ever: she had three fences down and ran out in the middle of the triple combination.

"An eventful round there for Linda Gorham on Glorious Girl," came the voice of the commentator. "Fifteen faults."

At least he didn't have to fear rounds like that on Cuaifeach. He hardly ever knocked a fence, he either jumped them or he didn't. Running out wasn't a habit with him either, he just stopped. At least he gave a clear indication of his intentions and that was something, Brian had said, it left you room to negotiate before coming up to the fence. In all, Cuaifeach was a dead honest pony and he behaved very well on a course. It wasn't really his fault that each of the three competitions they had entered so far had ended in failure.

On the very first occasion, the stallion had jumped an impeccable clear round. Dominic had been justly proud of him, especially since only six of the fifteen riders had gone clear. But when it came to the second round, Cuaifeach refused to enter the ring. Forced into it, nothing in the world could induce him to even look at a fence, let alone jump it. He just kept turning his head in the direction of the pocket, pointing towards it with his nose as if he had something of utmost importance to tell them all. Dominic could be stubborn when things mattered a lot to him, but with Cuaifeach he had to admit himself defeated; the stallion was just as stubborn, and a great deal stronger. It was heart-breaking to have to leave the arena with a pony he knew could make it, much worse than having the opposite problem, like the girl with the fifteen faults.

From the demonstrative way Cuaifeach attacked his feed bucket in the trailer, Dominic immediately knew what was wrong. They had conditioned him to jump a clear round in return for a bucket of nuts. Now they had suddenly moved the goal posts and asked him to do twice as much before handing over the reward due to him. No wonder Cuaifeach refused. He was a stallion who stuck to his bargains and expected others to do the same.

In the weeks that followed, the training pattern was successively modified, so that Cuaifeach had to achieve two clear rounds before being reunited with his bucket. He grudgingly accepted the change of policy.

Next in turn was a skewbald ridden by a small boy. The pony looked very unwilling, ears glued back, nose stuck right out so that his head was parallel to the ground. Reluctantly he jumped one fence after another—you could almost hear him groaning in protest. To everyone's surprise he went clear.

Cuaifeach's second competition had been even more of a mishap. Once again he had cleared the first round and, reconditioned, agreed to enter a second time. He jumped like a hare, finished high over a triple bar and left the ring with a flourish, oblivious of his rider's desperate attempts to turn him back. They still had two fences to go. The stallion was delighted with his splendid performance, but, nonetheless, they were eliminated.

Only one more pony to go before Cuaifeach, a plain grey gelding ridden by a girl much too tall for him. It's funny, Dominic thought, how carefully they measure the ponies before they are allowed to compete, but there's no question of measuring the riders.

He took up his position just inside the gate, feeling the mounting excitement in his muscles, the heavy beating of his heart. Make those nerves work for you, Brian kept saying. They are the worst thing you can have fighting against you!

It could only have been nerves that caused the awful thing to happen the previous Sunday. The rider before them had two falls early on and so had been eliminated, and before Dominic realised what was happening, his and Cuaifeach's names were called out over the PA system. Startled, he dug his heels into the stallion's sides, and they went off like a thunderbolt, completing the course in record time without a single fault. Just as Dominic drew a deep sigh of relief, he heard the commentator's voice: "Dominic O'Neill on Cuaifeach, sadly eliminated for starting before the bell...."

To know that it had all been his fault, not the pony's, somehow made it much worse.

The grey gelding, having started by running out at the first fence, was making his way ponderously over the jumps, looking hesitantly at each one. His rider's long legs came in useful as she wrapped them around him to urge on the gelding. Landing after the last fence, finishing with only three faults, she hit him hard with the whip. She should, of course, have patted her pony for doing so well and very likely that was her intention. Another example of the funny tricks nerves played with them all.

Dominic's turn had come, but he took no chances, just waited cautiously by the gate for the sound of the bell. There it was. And there was the first fence—a spread consisting of a cross-pole and a vertical. He lined up his pony and they cleared it comfortably and went straight for number two, a red and white upright fence. The third was an oxer painted a vitriolic greenish yellow, but Cuaifeach didn't mind the colour, he jumped it happily and then turned obediently towards number four, a double parallel. They got the stride right and were now approaching the fifth fence. Another vertical, quite high, it needed a more settled approach. Cuaifeach listened, checked and jumped clear. After a tight left-hand turn, where he had to quickly change leg, the stallion took on the next fence, a single parallel. He came in a little too close and brushed the first pole with his front leg, Dominic could see it tremble as they went over. He looked back, his heart in his mouth, but thank goodness, it was still in place. Hurriedly now, he turned his pony to the right and aimed at fence number seven, a stile with huge white wings. Cuaifeach had never jumped a stile before but he was going so well, he merely took it in his stride, thinking, as it were, that some time had to be the first.

Only one, but the worst challenge of all remained: the triple combination. A parallel, a vertical and then another parallel, with awkward distances in between. Dominic had little experience of related distances and Cuaifeach even less. All he knew was that the approach was all-important. If you didn't get your stride right for the first, you'd had it. He concentrated hard, checked and checked again, and then Cuaifeach sailed through the air, bounced like a rubber ball between the fences and took off again.

They were clear! For the third momentous time in his life, Dominic heard the words, like the most beautiful music, ring out of the PA system: "A clear round for Dominic O'Neill on Cuaifeach." There was applause from the crowd and Cuaifeach, very pleased with himself, stopped to acknowledge it, like royalty.

Then they were in for another of those long waits that neither of them weathered very well. There were twenty-four more riders to go. When they finally were allowed in to inspect the course for the second round, both Dominic and Cuaifeach were suffering from a severe bout of acute overexcitement. Since there had been only one clear round before them, they were second to go. Limbs trembling with repressed tension, they watched the unwilling skewbald make a mess of his second round. The sequence had been altered, and Dominic followed the movements round the course to make sure he'd got it right. He could feel Cuaifeach beneath him like a coiled spring rearing to go and had to forcibly hold him back by the gate until the bell had gone for them. Then he urged the stallion forward, but he needn't have bothered; this pony needed no urging. He flew over the first, which was now a vertical, then over the second, a parallel, the third, the yellow oxer, the fourth, in and out he went like the whirlwind that had given him his name and Dominic thought, not so fast, not so fast, we're not against the clock, though we will be one day and by golly, by then we'll beat them all! Help! Where are we? Where is number five?

Cuaifeach wasn't waiting for instructions, he was heading straight towards the next fence, cleared it with a foot to spare and then sped towards the sixth and last. Only that wasn't the sixth fence at all, he was going for the wrong one....

Dominic tried to turn him right round before the irrevocable happened, but it was no good; the stallion was already taking off for it, and a second later they were over and clear.

"Sadly eliminated...." The words sounded painfully familiar.

Four weeks of excruciating hard work, and not a single point to show for it.

Not a single point to show his dad.

Friends Indeed

7

A moonless winter night in Connemara is what you'd call dark, as dark as anything on this earth. Once the scattered lights of the cottages and bungalows go out, the countryside is sunk into a blackness so complete that you'd have to be blind to find your way through it. Few people venture out at night unless safely ensconced in motor-cars; those who do make sure they have something to light them. A Connemara man carries his torch everywhere, like a lady her handbag, and he could be in deep trouble whenever the batteries run out.

When Julia drove up in front of her cottage at three o'clock in the morning, she left her headlights on as usual to be able to locate the house. In the beginning she had made the mistake of switching them off and had ended up getting lost between the car and the front door. It was amazing how shapes and distances, even those you knew as well as the back of your hand, somehow were not the same in the darkness.

However, this time she needn't have bothered. The garda patrol car was right behind her, and the instant it pulled up the two gardaí leapt out of the car waving powerful police torches, sweeping their beams over garden and walls, coming to rest on Julia's front door. It was hanging on its hinges, the lock broken, just as she had told them. The men exchanged a glance and a nod. No doubt about it, this was a forced entry.

For a moment they stood stock still listening for sounds, but there was nothing except for the whining noise over the bog, the foreboding of a severe storm. Then, suddenly, one of the gardaí picked up a rustle in the field behind the house. He ran to the wall and vaulted over it like a hurdler, followed by the other man who, older and more thickset, took a little longer to negotiate the high stone wall. By the time Julia was out of her car, they were both in the field and she could hear a strange carfuffle going on in there.

"Stop!" she cried, running towards the beams of light swaying wildly with their movements. "Don't! You're upsetting them!"

There was a thud followed by a muttered curse and then one of the light beams settled on the ground, lighting an oblong streak of sodden grass in front of it. Before long, however, the garda was back on his feet, the beam once more on the move. Julia shouted for all she was worth for them to come back, to give up pursuing her yearling colts. The latter, understandably, had taken exception to having their nightly peace disturbed by two burly gardaí and were galloping around in a frenzy. Any minute now, Julia thought, they would take a leaf out of their father's book, jump the wall and go visiting Jim Lydon's prize-winning mares. She had hoped and prayed that such pleasures would remain undisclosed to them until they were safely despatched to England.

All the trouble it would bring, keeping them confined, all the work of housing three hyperactive colts in a stable too small for them. All that she had hoped to avoid.... She groaned inwardly. It wasn't as if she didn't have enough on her plate already.

Fortunately, before the inevitable happened, the colts decided on a counterattack. Being their father's sons, they weren't the faint-hearted kind and soon saw to it that the two gardaí had to scramble over the wall for safety. At least that should satisfy them that there were no burglars in the field, Julia thought to herself. It was highly unlikely anyhow that the thieves would still be hanging around. She had been out since nine o'clock and it was half past one when she returned home to find her front door forced open. She had driven straight to the Clifden garda station to report the burglary, but had to wait for over an hour before the one patrol car had been located and called in. Whoever had raided her cottage would be far away by now.

While the gardaí went on to search the garden, Julia steeled herself for whatever was waiting indoors. Would the place be ransacked, her most cherished belongings gone? This would never have happened if Cuaifeach had still been here, she reflected sadly. He wouldn't have let anyone through the gate. In his capacity as a guard dog, he had been more effective than the most ferocious alsatian.

A little later she and the gardaí were sitting by her kitchen table. The thickset man, in a somewhat grumpy mood, was writing in a notebook.

"And you're sure nothing is missing?" he asked for a second time.

"Quite sure," Julia replied. On the garda's instruction she had checked everything there was worth stealing: the little jewellery she kept in the cottage, television, stereo, camera. "They don't seem to have taken anything. When you live alone it's easy to keep track of your possessions."

"Did you tell anyone you'd be out tonight?" the younger man enquired. This drew a vexed look from his colleague, as if he thought it quite enough for one of them to conduct the enquiries. He was still put out about being lured into the field and chased around by ponies.

"Anyone could have figured that out" was Julia's reply. "I went to a dinner and dance at Maam Cross in aid of the Roundstone Pony Show. There was a big crowd there—some three hundred people—all involved with ponies."

"Did you go on your own?"

"What has that got to do with it?" the grumpy garda interrupted his colleague.

"I met up with a friend of mine, Wilfrid Smith-

Andrews. He works for the Department of Agriculture."

"Perhaps you disturbed them when you came back?" the younger garda suggested.

"That wouldn't have stopped them since I went off again straight away."

The older garda had got up and was pacing thoughtfully to and fro in the kitchen, seemingly in pursuit of quite a different line of thought.

"In my experience," he said slowly after a while, "there are more mischief-makers than thieves in this part of the country. It appears to me that someone may have wanted to annoy you more than anything else, scare you perhaps.... I mean, since they had every opportunity to take what they wanted and yet didn't touch anything. There must have been a different motive."

Julia's grim expression was enough to indicate that he was on the right track.

"You've had trouble before, haven't you?" he asked gently.

She drew a deep sigh and nodded in agreement. "It's been going on for some time."

It was all to do with the ponies, she told them, her efforts to help local breeders get better prices for their youngstock. The first telephone call had come in the middle of the night, shortly after she announced her intentions at a social in Clifden. It was a man with a local accent. "Keep your hands off the ponies," he said. "The likes of you are not wanted here." Then he rang again a few days later, the same man—she recognised his voice. This time he was more threatening. He asked her did she know what happened to people who didn't heed warnings? After that she had stopped answering the phone at night, though it rang a couple of times.

Then another call had come in the afternoon, only a few days earlier. "You've been warned," the man said, and "you're going to regret this."

"Have you any idea who it might be?" the thickset garda asked her.

"No. It could be anyone. Anyone who doesn't like what I'm doing."

"And is that the end of it?"

Julia pulled a piece of paper out of her handbag.

"I thought I heard footsteps in the garden one night. I nearly rang the station, but nothing else happened, so I told myself it must have been my imagination. But in the morning I found this. It had been pushed under my back door."

She handed the garda a page torn out of a school exercise book. On it was printed in large black letters: "GO BACK TO ENGLAND WHILE YOU'RE STILL ABLE."

"You didn't report it?" the older garda asked.

"There didn't seem much point."

"Can I keep this?"

"Is there anything you can do?" Julia asked doubtfully.

The garda gave her a fatherly smile, his grumpiness forgotten. "We live in a closed community. Word travels fast, especially along unofficial lines. Leave it to us, don't let them get the better of you. As for the phone calls, we'll soon put a stop to them."

He produced a police whistle from his pocket.

"The next time your telephone rings in the middle of the night, pick up the receiver and blow long and hard into it. I can guarantee that your friend won't ring again."

He got up and put his notebook away.

"We'll make a few enquiries," he said. "I honestly don't believe that you have much to worry about. Is there a bolt on that door?"

As they left, he smiled and winked at her. "Don't forget the whistle."

Julia smiled back. "I can't wait to use it."

The opportunity presented itself sooner than she had expected. The telephone rang only minutes after the red rear lights of the patrol car had vanished around the bend. Armed with the police whistle, drawing a deep breath, Julia lifted the receiver and did as she had been advised, blew long and hard into it. It brought her a rare vicious pleasure to hear the pathetic moaning at the other end of the line. The image of her antagonist clutching his ear in agony brought a smile of cruel satisfaction to her lips. Serves you right, she thought. But then came a feeble voice: "Julia...are you all right?"

"Wilfrid!" she exclaimed.

"What happened?" he wailed.

"Oh Wilfrid, darling, I'm so sorry. I didn't think it was you."

Nothing but silence emitted from his end.

"Wilfrid! Are you there?"

"You called me darling," he stated in a voice next

to normal, as if the mere fact had been enough to dispel both pain and anxiety.

"Did I?" said Julia. "I just wanted to say I didn't mean to hurt your ear. Is it very painful?"

"What about you?" Wilfrid wanted to know. "I rang before to check that you were home safely but there was no reply. I got worried. Tell me, what's going on?"

Julia suddenly felt exhausted.

"I'm fine," she said. "We'll talk tomorrow. Sleep well, if you can for that ear."

It didn't seem to bother him all that much.

"Good night," he said. *"Darling."*

***

The storm broke in the early morning and Julia was woken up by the howling in the chimney, the rattling of roof tiles over her head, the lashing of rain on the windowpanes. She burrowed deep into the bed-clothes thinking this was the kind of day when any sensible person would stay indoors, make up a roaring big fire and sit in front of it drinking cups of tea and reading a good book.

No such luxury for her, though. She had arranged to go down to South Connemara to view some ponies. At the dance the previous night a couple of men and one woman had approached her in turn, discreetly as always, mumbling invitations to come and see what they had on offer. Julia wished she could forget all about it, but knew she had to go. So far she had managed to secure no more than a dozen suitable ponies, and the only way she'd ever get out of this troublesome situation was by completing the job in hand. However difficult it had proved to be, there was no other way. Her life wouldn't revert to normal until the lorry-load of ponies was on its way to England.

When she had first embarked on the task of putting this deal together, it had all seemed dead simple. For one thing, the English customers were the nicest of people, as straight as they come and, like most knowledgeable buyers, more concerned with obtaining good quality than striking a bargain. They had set down on paper exactly what they were after and what they did not like to see in a pony. Specified as desirable traits were a good sloping shoulder, well-pronounced withers, a free elbow and a good length of rein plus, of course, a beautiful head, strong clean legs and vigorous movement. The list of undesirables included things like cow hocks and dishing legs, choppy strides and weak hindquarters, roman noses and piggy eyes. On the whole, their idea of a good mount closely matched Julia's own. Moreover, countless ponies in Connemara fitted this bill. It summed up all that the breed was renowned for.

Her task really couldn't have been easier. All she had to do was put together a short-list of suitable ponies. She didn't even have to take responsibility for the selection. Once her job was done, the customers planned to come over themselves to make the final decisions.

But nothing is ever as simple and straightforward as you imagine, especially in pony circles in Connemara. Even disregarding things like telephone terror, nightly prowlers, anonymous letters and break-ins, Julia was beginning to feel that she had let herself in for more than she could comfortably handle.

One thing that she couldn't for her life understand was the reluctance of many people to have any dealings with her at all. It was as if they didn't trust her, though there was no way they could possibly be cheated. Everyone who sold a pony would receive the full payment in cash before handing it over, at a price agreed by themselves beforehand.

Conversely, there were those who were only too willing to deal. So willing, in fact, that they deliberately misled her, filled her up with faulty information just to secure a sale. She had been assured that ponies were four years old when they were nine, fourteen-two when they were thirteen-three, geldings when they were colts, barren when they were in foal. It meant she had to check every single detail, that is, the details that were possible to check. And this was easier said than done, for passports were frequently "mislaid" or even missing. Only when she declared that there would be no negotiation until she had seen the pony's papers, were they reluctantly produced.

Prices were another tricky matter. With the

customers prepared to pay a good price for a good product, Julia hadn't foreseen any problems there. After all, the breeders would get paid way above what they were used to; that was the whole object of the exercise. But this soon went to people's heads, particularly when reports of Julia's deals started to circulate in the locality. There was the sweet old man who had offered her a lovely two-year-old filly, shyly requesting three hundred pounds for her.

"I'd like to put her on my list," Julia had said, "but not at three hundred."

"Oh well," the old boy said resignedly. "Two hundred then. Whatever you think."

"You should get at least five-fifty," said Julia. "That's what she's worth."

On another occasion two young brothers had showed her a rangy three-year-old gelding, one of them declaring solemnly that they wanted seven hundred pounds for him, whereupon they both broke into uncontrollable fits of giggles behind her back.

"That's fine with me," Julia retorted. "Seven hundred seems a fair price for him."

The brothers' faces dropped as if she had poured a bucket of cold water over them. As she left, she heard one of them hissing to the other, "I told you we should have asked a thousand. That one doesn't mind what she's paying."

However, it soon got to the stage where no-one quoted her less than four figures for anything possessing four hooves and a tail. She faced tough negotiations to bring prices down to a realistic level, a level which was still above what people expected. Moreover, her favourable deals were arousing much envy and competition, causing extra complications as far as Julia was concerned.

One mean-looking man had accosted her one day in McWilliams' supermarket in Ballyconneely.

"I hear you're buying Pat Kieran's mare," he said. "I hope he told you she's got laryngitis."

"Are you sure of that?" Julia enquired. The pony had showed no sign of having anything wrong with her throat. Come to think of it, was it even possible for a horse to suffer from laryngitis?

"Yeah," the man reaffirmed. "Bad laryngitis she has. All four hooves."

"You mean 'laminitis'," Julia stated, alarmed. Although she had never seen a pony in Connemara with laminitis—it was an ailment associated with rich grasslands—it was a serious enough disorder to warrant investigation.

Pat Kieran's reaction was one of such overpowering rage that Julia feared he would attack her for bringing such tidings. "Who told you this?" he growled, a murderous glint in his eyes. "Just give me his name, so I can go and break his bloody neck!"

"Don't take it to heart," Julia said in a futile effort to calm him down. "Just let me check her hooves."

"My mare doesn't need her hooves checking," the man snapped furiously. "It's you need your head examined, listening to scum like that. I have a fair idea who he is, and I'll tell you this: it's jealous he is for not being able to sell you his own mangy old mare. That's one you wouldn't have if he threw her after you!"

All Julia could do in the circumstances was make a mental note to have all hooves specially checked by the vet prior to delivery. He'd have to check a few other things as well, the way things were going.

What a relief it would be when all this was over!

In the late morning she drove south through the wind and rain, along the coast and across bogs into the vast stony tracts of South Connemara. This was a country very different from the relatively prosperous parts around Clifden. The fields were poor and marshy, the small cottages few and far between, the roads, winding their way between lakes and sea inlets, narrow and badly maintained. The directions she had were as vague as could be expected of any directions given at a party well after midnight, but at least she had the name of one of the men and knew that he was a plumber. After an hour of driving along roads that all looked the same, guided along only by the odd unintelligible sign in Irish, the language of the Gaeltacht, she realised that she was hopelessly lost. When at last she spotted a cottage, she stopped to ask the way. A large, brusque-looking woman opened the door to her knock. Julia asked if she knew Johnny Coyne, the plumber?

"Do I know Johnny Coyne?" the woman shouted, affronted.

No more was volunteered in the way of a reply.

"I wonder where I can find him," Julia added, undaunted.

"Well so do I!" the woman cried. "Didn't he start on my bathroom four months ago, and since then there's been no sign of him! Come in and see for yourself!"

She motioned Julia indoors and flung open a door to a poky little room off the kitchen. Most of the floor space was taken up by a bath-tub covered by a thick layer of dust. From the wall two unconnected pipes gaped at them.

"The nieces from America were coming over," the woman explained in a voice full of grievance. "We wanted to have a bathroom all ready for them. But now they've been and gone, and thanks to your man this was all we had to show for ourselves."

Though she would much rather have turned straight back to Errislannan, Julia drove on through the bleak landscape, about as barren and deserted as the surface of the moon. Here and there, on either side of the road, ponies were picking amongst the rocks, thin and bedraggled-looking, but nevertheless bearing the quality hallmark of the Connemara breed. It was said that many of the old well-proven bloodlines were still going strong in this remote area, thanks to the fact that breeding and trading here had been less intense than in other places.

However endless the road seemed, it had to end somewhere, she said to herself and, sure enough, she eventually found herself in Carraroe, a small town at the south-western tip of Connemara. Checking her notes she saw that she wasn't far from the woman she was going to see. Her directions had been more specific and they brought her down a small boreen towards the sea, ending in a small field, across which was a tiny thatched cottage with wisps of smoke wafting from the chimney.

Julia crossed the field, bowing her head against the wind that came blasting in from the Atlantic, no shelter in sight. The woman she had met at the dance came out to meet her and showed her where to climb the stone wall surrounding her little garden since there was no gate. She was a small middle-aged woman in a bright red track suit, a happy smile imprinted on her face, as if no hardship, no privation would ever be strong enough to erase it.

She invited her guest into the cottage, just the one room with an earth floor and an open fire over which a huge pot of potatoes was boiling. A number of children, from toddlers to teenagers, seemed to be filling up every available space. They were standing, sitting or crawling, playing, reading or drawing. The woman opened her hands in a gesture to take in the whole interior.

"As you see, we haven't got much. You can tell your friend that. He won't get anything out of us."

Julia looked at her, baffled.

"My husband used to fish," the woman continued, "but he was struck down with rheumatoid arthritis, and now we only have the social security. So there'll be no tax due, even if you buy our ponies."

"I'm sorry," Julia said, "but I don't know what you're talking about."

The woman smiled her warm smile at her. "You

don't have to pretend with us. We know all about it."

"All about what?" Julia asked, a horrible suspicion beginning to form in her mind.

The woman's response confirmed it. "Everybody knows you're in league with that taxman you go around with. The one that goes about asking questions."

"Is that what they say about me? That I inform on the people I deal with?"

"And why shouldn't you?" the woman said good-humouredly. "I mean, if they pay you that well—wouldn't anyone?"

"It's a lie," Julia protested. "I imagine it's been put around by people trying to stop me. Believe me, not a word of it is true."

But the woman just kept smiling. Then she went out and pointed to two small dots on the horizon: the ponies she wanted to sell. Julia prepared herself for a long, stormy hike across the mountain, but when the woman called out in a lovely, clear voice, the kind that carries across the bog, the ponies flung themselves headlong across the rough terrain, galloping sure-footedly non-stop until they stood in front of their owner. They were small and scruffy, stunted from poor nutrition, but they looked sturdy enough and, with their thick winter coats and affectionate demeanour, were more like a pair of cuddly teddy bears than ponies. Two of the children were summoned to ride them bareback around the field. It didn't take Julia long to establish that they had everything you could wish for in a small children's pony. She told the woman that she would offer them to her customers at six hundred pounds for the two.

"Six hundred!" the woman said wistfully, her smile momentarily gone. "That would pay for a TV...and the electricity to go with it! Oh if only it were possible, we'd be blessing you every time we watch 'Glenroe'."

"Won't you miss them?" Julia asked, seeing one of the ponies nuzzling her devotedly.

"We will," said the woman. "We'll miss them something fearful, it will be like sending the older children to work abroad. But that's life, sure. You can't hold them back from doing better."

As Julia got back into her car, the woman and her children all saw her off, waving and beaming, and the woman called out: "You can tell your friend all about us. I don't mind at all!" Her smile was as broad as ever.

8

Roc O'Neill had never shared or understood his son's interest in riding, and so he received the news that Dominic had entered Cuaifeach for a cross-country competition the following weekend with no more enthusiasm than if he had proposed to take Rosie for a hack down the road. It was only a day or so later that Roc suddenly remembered the time when, out of sheer curiosity, he had watched such an event at the Olympic Games in Montreal. Memories flashed through his mind of intrepid horses going hell for leather across a rough track, hurling themselves over formidable fences in valiant defiance of gravity and self-preservation; glamorous, mud-spattered contestants smiling proudly as they were given their prizes. Was this the way his son, his own timid little boy, was going? In his mind's eye Roc caught a brief glimpse of Dominic in colourful garb and silk-covered skull-cap, holding out his hand to receive a gold medal, just like the one he himself treasured more than any of his other possessions.

Ah, for the glory of sport! How dull and empty life

was without it. Roc had never stopped hankering for the excitement of days gone by. The quest of victory had guided his every move, urged him on like a shining golden carrot in front of a starved donkey. Once tasted it became an addiction, nothing ever compared to it. The sweetest thrill life could offer was that of pitching your own best skills against those of others, in the titillating assumption that you were going to win. If there was one experience Roc wished he could grant his son, that was it.

He hadn't thought the lad had it in him. His retiring ways and lanky physique—traits inherited, needless to say, from his wife's side of the family— did not exactly make for the dynamics inherent in a good sportsman. But there must be more to him than meets the eye, Roc thought smugly. Blood is obviously thicker than water.

Dominic's heart sank right into his boots when his father rang up to congratulate him on the forthcoming cross-country competition and inform him that he intended to come along to cheer him on. He could have kicked himself for writing to his dad about the forthcoming event and kicked himself even harder for putting on all that false bravado. He often fell into that trap when communicating with his father; it was as if he had a constant need to present himself as better and braver than he really was. The idea, presumably, was to gain his father's attention and approval. Well, if that was so, he had certainly succeeded this time. Only he wished to God that he hadn't.

The cross-country competition was not something Dominic was looking forward to. To tell the truth, which he had done to no-one, the mere thought of it made his knees go wobbly. Show-jumping was one thing. He enjoyed the skill and precision it involved, but as for galloping at breakneck speed over huge fences cross-country...Dominic shuddered. He couldn't imagine anything more daunting.

He had agreed to enter only because Brian had insisted, adamant that it was exactly what Cuaifeach needed. The stallion was getting worse, not better, in the showjumping arena. He played up, refused fences he had previously taken in his stride and knocked quite a few of those he agreed to jump. According to Brian, he was doing it out of sheer recalcitrance. Apparently it wasn't uncommon in green ponies to go through such periods, it was a form of rebelling against the strict discipline of the show ring. But it had to be stamped on without delay, Brian warned, and the best way to overcome the problem was to get Cuaifeach to jump something entirely different, such as a cross-country course. With all the excitement and speed of such an event, the pony would soon forget all about wayward resistance.

"Perhaps he just needs a little rest?" Dominic had suggested diffidently, not wanting to let on that he was lacking in guts.

But Brian dismissed the idea outright. "That would be the ruin of him altogether. Like telling him, if it doesn't suit him to perform, he doesn't have to."

And so, at a loss for a better argument, Dominic had let himself be talked into it. Having got this far, he knew he had to go through with it, regardless of his own secret reservations. But the one thing he could have done without was the extra pressure of having his father present.

For a while it looked as though the powers that be were on his side because it rained steadily for two days, and the going became so soft there was talk of having to cancel the Sunday competition. Dominic looked through the window at the heavy downpour outside, savouring the relief it would bring him. However, on the Saturday the rain stopped abruptly and high winds helped dry out the ground so that it became possible—just—to hold the event as scheduled.

Walking the course on the day, Dominic couldn't believe that fences such as these could be jumped at all. Brian had briefed him thoroughly on sheep troughs and tables, coffins and tiger-traps, but nothing could have prepared him for the real thing. To make things worse, when they got Cuaifeach out of the trailer and mounted him, it became apparent that the stallion was every bit as tense and uneasy as he was himself. Unlike himself, however, Cuaifeach did nothing to conceal the fact. He didn't stand still for a moment, pranced on his toes, jogged around in circles and, at one time, even tried to get up on his hind legs. He looked restlessly from the first fence to a couple of mares nearby, as if he wasn't sure which challenge was the greater and which one he was to tackle first. After all, spring was in the air and the mating season not far away.

As many eyes turned to watch him and his restive mount, Dominic wished he had been dressed in something less ostentatious. His skull-cap and top, as well as the pony's matching overgirth, were a blazing emerald and fuchsia, enough you would have thought to scare any horse. Roc had taken him to a shop specialising in cross-country equipment the previous day and had bought him a whole new outfit. To begin with, his father had insisted on green and orange, joking with the assistant, saying that you might as well start as you intended to end, wearing the colours of your country. Dominic had asked for something more muted, but the assistant had said all cross-country clothes were in such dazzling colours. The idea was to make the rider clearly visible from a distance.

Clearly visible.... You could say that again. Dominic felt he stood out like a beacon against the pale sky. If the choice had been his, he would have appeared no more conspicuous than a grey mouse. He probably looked like one anyway, a pathetic grey little mouse decked out in finery.

After Cuaifeach had tried to rear up a second time, Brian told Dominic to pinch the skin on the pony's shoulder, just hold it there between his thumb and forefinger and see what happened. Amazingly, Cuaifeach settled down somewhat. An old trick, Brian said modestly, but Dominic thought, how on earth am I going to jump cross-country fences with my thumb and forefinger pinching his shoulder?

The warm-up area was crowded with competitors cantering around in supreme confidence, popping over the thick fallen tree-trunk in the middle with a minimum of fuss. Cuaifeach, however, threatened to go berserk when Dominic tried to get him over the practice fence. The boy didn't realise that on a windy day, trees to a Connemara pony are Bad News whether lying down or standing up, like those in the wood surrounding the course. Much of the stallion's fretfulness was in fact due to the large number of trees around him. After all, he came from a place where trees are few and far between and very much at the mercy of ferocious elements. Even a foal in Connemara knows that, with a high wind blowing, trees can't be trusted; only a fool would go anywhere near them.

Dominic galloped for five minutes around the edge of the ring. It was all he could do in the circumstances, and at the end of the five minutes, at least Cuaifeach was tired enough to draw breath.

Just as the riders were gathering in the area between the car park and the starting-box, Roc chose to arrive. As usual he drove up in his expensive sports car at full speed and showed off by braking suddenly, making the mud splash all over the place. This trick never failed to attract attention, and this day the effect was spectacular. Two of the ponies, who had been unfortunate enough to linger close by, flew in the air, took off and crashed right into a group of other competitors. It could have ended in a major disaster, but luckily the riders were soon able to bring their ponies back under control. Nonetheless, Roc was met by some very dirty looks when he got out of the car, smiling affably.

Dominic was overcome with embarrassment. It was a new sensation; he was normally, like most people, in considerable awe of his famous father. But in this place Roc somehow didn't fit in. He was like a fish out of water—a swimmer out of water—Dominic corrected himself. For one thing, his clothes were all wrong. He was wearing a loud yellow blazer with tartan checks, as if it was he who had to be seen over a distance. And he walked along as if he owned the place, expecting riders to move out of his path. He slapped Brian chummily on the back, pointing at Cuaifeach and braying in a voice as loud as his blazer, so that no-one could miss a word of it, "The stallion is looking grand, Brian. Much more *competitive* than I remember him. You sure have done wonders, both with him and the boy!"

To Roc, the word "competitive" was about the greatest compliment he could pay anyone, but as all heads turned in the direction of Cuaifeach and his rider, Dominic wished a big hole would open in the ground for him to sink through. It was quite enough to be facing his first ever cross-country competition astride a raving mad stallion. He didn't need this kind of torment on top.

Roc was eyeing his son with the kind of smug paternal approval that would have delighted the boy any other day of the year, but now it only made him feel wretched, because he knew he couldn't possibly live up to his father's expectations. His own aspirations stopped at getting over the course alive. Brian must have seen the look of exasperation on his face, for he said in a discreet, comforting tone of voice, "Don't worry about him."

At first Dominic thought he was referring to Roc, but then Brian continued: "All stallions get a bit hyped up at this time of year, with the hormones flowing freely. Once you get started, though, you'll find that pent-up energy very useful."

Sure. Easy for him to say.

As the first competitor entered the starting-box, Brian took his guest off to find a good vantage-point from which he could see as many fences as possible. Dominic heaved a sigh of relief. Being number eleven, he had half an hour's excruciating wait ahead of him, and it would be better spent without the cheery company of his father.

One by one the riders went off over the first fence, a short straight pole over bales of straw. They all cleared it easily before vanishing into the hinterland of fences beyond. Dominic waited nervously, clutching the skin on Cuaifeach's shoulder, attracting a few condescending glances from other riders who did not have to resort to such tricks. Waiting and watching, feeling slightly better at the sight of other ponies getting restless and misbehaving, he soon forgot the time, and all of a sudden it was his turn to trot over to the starting-box. The stallion's back felt as hard as a board underneath him, and his movements were stiff and jerky.

Cuaifeach was never usually like that, Dominic reflected, and then suddenly it occurred to him that perhaps it was his own lack of confidence that had communicated itself to his mount. He had heard somewhere that animals can smell fear in others. If that was so, he was letting his pony down badly by allowing fear to get a hold of him. The poor beast knew even less than he did about cross-country competitions, he was looking to his rider for encouragement and support, and so far he had got neither.

Brian returned to see if he needed help going into the starting-box, but Cuaifeach amazingly went straight in and then agreed to stand there quietly for a whole minute. Dominic had the feeling that the stallion was, more than anything, bewildered. "I'm sorry," he whispered out of Brian's hearing, patting the pony's shoulder. "I haven't exactly made it easier for you. But I'll help you now. We'll get it right, you and I together."

As he talked to him, the stallion's ears shot forward, for the first time that day, and he seemed to relax a little.

"Three-two-one-go! called the starter, adding "Good luck!" as if he thought the boy could do with it.

Cuaifeach got off to a good start and jumped the first fence without problems. Boosted by this achievement, they took the next three in rapid succession: a small coffin, a double straight and a straight pole. Each time they jumped, it seemed that some of the awful tension left both their bodies. If we go on like this, Dominic said to himself, we might even start enjoying ourselves towards the end.

Number five was a straight pole before water and at the sight of it Cuaifeach suddenly hesitated, remembering what his mother had taught him about carefully smelling any waterlogged area before stepping into it. In Connemara there are bog-holes deep enough for a pony to drown in, or even worse, the mire may grab hold of his hooves and mercilessly suck him down. Only by using his nose can a pony assess the safety of the ground underneath the watery surface. And so, Cuaifeach did what any sensible Connemara would do in a similar situation: he stopped short to sniff the water before jumping into it.

Sadly, his rider was unprepared for the sudden stop. He went over the pole and into the ice cold muddy water while his mount was still busy sniffing.

When Dominic got to his feet, he found the pony staring at him over the pole, looking as if he were debating whether or not to jump in after him. Just as the boy came back to remount him, Cuaifeach made up his mind and sprang in the air, landing square in the middle of the pool. Angrily, the boy waded in after him, but the pony just turned and splashed exuberantly with his front hooves, sending cascades of water over his friend, as if he didn't think he was quite wet enough. He looked almost as if he was laughing, which in a way, he was. Playing in water had been his favourite pastime when he was a wild young colt on an island off the west coast, and it brought back memories of days when all had been fun and freedom, none of this wretched hard work and discipline.

Dominic, knowing nothing about this, could be forgiven for not sharing the joke. In fact, the sight of the stallion so delighted with himself made him so furious he forgot all about being afraid. He jumped on his back and dug his heels in with such fervour that Cuaifeach was taken unawares and before either of them quite knew what was happening, they had sailed through the next nine fences: drops and banks, a sheep trough, a bullfinch and finally a table, the fence Brian had warned him about as being the most treacherous of all.

But number sixteen was a double water jump, and by now Cuaifeach was having such a good time he wouldn't let anything stop him having another go at his own personal brand of horseplay. Recalling the previous pool as being perfectly safe, he didn't even stop to sniff this time. Dominic, half expecting trouble, closed his legs tight on the pony's sides and took a firm grip of his mouth, but there is really very little a rider can do to stop a pony hell-bent on plunging himself into a pool of water and then staying there. At least this time he didn't fall off, though he got soaked to the skin once more by water splashing all over him. All he needed now was to get the stallion to go on, but alas, Cuaifeach had no such intentions. He skipped back and forth, swivelled around, leapt high, but would not go forward. Having found his favoured spot in this giant playground, he was no more inclined to leave it than a child who has discovered the most thrilling attraction at a funfair.

Dominic raised his whip. So far he had never used it on Cuaifeach. Doreen had warned him that beating her pony would get him nowhere, but that was typical girl-talk. She had never been caught in the middle of a cross-country course with a pony refusing to budge. Brian, for his part, had taught him that the only place to chastise a stallion was below the knee, but that wasn't easy when he was standing in two feet of water. Dominic had little choice; he gave the pony a good wallop on his right flank. It had little effect. For one thing, Cuaifeach was pretty impervious to pain when something else was occupying his mind, and secondly, the whip brushed the surface of the water, which significantly reduced its impact. Dominic had the creepy feeling that everyone was looking at him and laughing and he hit the pony furiously once more, on the shoulder, with all the power generated by anger and frustration. This time he was more successful; Cuaifeach acknowledged it, too. Only, in his view corporal punishment was not part of the agreement he had entered into with this boy. He retaliated by bucking Dominic right back into the water, before putting his head down for a long refreshing drink.

Two officials were by now approaching the fence to clear it before the next competitor was due to jump. One of them caught Cuaifeach by the reins, pulled him away and then helped the boy, dripping with water, to get back into the saddle. It was then that Dominic suddenly remembered his father, he must have been watching all this. The thought made him so mortified he just clenched his teeth and urged the pony on grimly. He was very annoyed with Cuaifeach, all the affection for him was gone. How could he ever again feel affection for an animal which had made him look such a fool in front of his dad?

Just to show he was well able to do it, Cuaifeach jumped the remaining few fences with style and ease, except for the tiger-trap, which he refused four times, but since they must have been eliminated anyhow, it made little difference.

Brian was nowhere to be seen, and Dominic had to dismount and put Cuaifeach away on his own. Eventually he found his coach in the middle of giving Roc an elaborate explanation of the rules for cross-country competitions. It sounded very much as if he was making excuses for his charge's dismal failure. When he came up to join them, Roc turned and stared aghast at his son, whose appearance had more in common with a drowned rat than the valiant gold-medallist of his imagination. But then, reminding himself of the sportsman's code, he gave another cheerful smile and put a friendly arm around the boy's shoulders, though he quickly withdrew it again when he noticed how wet his blazer got.

"Never mind," he said in the patronising voice that Dominic so hated, since it was always applied to cover up Roc's own disappointment in his son. "The main thing is that you enjoyed yourself."

Dominic gave him a look so resentful it made his father flinch.

"Enjoyed myself?" the boy snapped. "You must be joking!"

9

Raftery's Rest in Craughwell is a favourite haunt of the famous Galway Blazers, or the County Galway Hunt, as it is officially known. To anyone entering the roadside inn, the hunting connection is obvious, from the traditional tally-ho prints on the walls to the life-size fox sitting cross-legged on the bar dressed in a scarlet coat, white stock and black riding boots.

It was a Saturday in late February, and the hunt was gathering that morning for one of the last meets of the season in Raftery's car park. As usual at weekends, the meet had attracted a large crowd: horses and riders, spectators and those who intended to follow the hunt on foot. Among the latter were Doreen and Julia.

The girl had been thrilled when Julia asked her to come along. She herself had an appointment to see Bill Ryan, the field-master, later that day. He had told her that Dominic and Cuaifeach were going hunting with him, and so she had decided to kill two birds with one stone.

Like most Connemara people, Doreen was not at all familiar with hunting. There were certainly enough foxes around her part of the country, but with the mountains and bogs everywhere, you couldn't possibly ride to hounds over it. Besides, fox-hunting was traditionally associated with the landed gentry and their well-run estates, and there were precious few of those west of Lough Corrib. In days gone by, Connemara girls who married into the gentry of the eastern counties were at a terrible disadvantage because they were not used to hunting. It really is something you have to grow up with to fully appreciate, even though, nowadays, many adults take it up because they can afford it and believe it a smart thing to be doing. How much they enjoy it, though, is an open question.

Fancy having a father who fixed you up for a day's hunting just like that, Doreen thought to herself. She had heard that hunting cost a fortune. But Dominic's dad had become very generous of late. That was why Cuaifeach was going home. Roc O'Neill had finally agreed that it was time his son had "something decent" to ride. As if Cuaifeach wasn't good enough for him! Oh well, Doreen mused, it suits me fine to get him back again. She had missed him a lot, although her ankle had been slow in healing and she hadn't been able to ride until only recently.

She watched in amazement the scene unfolding in front of her. Never before had she seen so many horses together, it must be well over seventy. They were beautiful, some of them huge—seventeen hands or more—and all, like their riders, perfectly turned out, though she noticed that quite a few were equipped with pelham bits and curb chains, dropped nosebands and martingales. They obviously took some riding. Over in a corner she spotted a number of small, shaggy, tough-looking ponies, mounted by young boys and girls who looked as if they'd never been afraid of anything in their lives and probably never would be.

And then there was Cuaifeach. Her own stallion.... She hardly recognised him at first, he had put on so much weight and was clipped all over. He looked absolutely gorgeous, no other horse compared with him. She said as much to Julia, who laughed and said, "Don't you know, it's all in the eye of the beholder."

She went up to her pony in some trepidation. What if he didn't recognise her or didn't care about her any more? He might have switched his allegiance to Dominic for good. But she had underestimated her stallion's sense of loyalty. He only had to hear her voice to start whickering excitedly, and then he gave her a thorough sniffing, as if only her delicious scent could convince him that it was really her and not some apparition. She put her arms around his neck and felt him heaving some deep contented sighs. When she finally stepped back, he went after her as if he wanted to say, I may have someone else on my back, but you are still the one I follow.

"All right, Cuaifeach," she said. "It won't be long now."

Dominic had changed even more than the pony in the two months they'd been together. His attractive, diffident smile had been replaced by a more serious, resigned look, as if he had suddenly grown much older.

"Are you feeling nervous?" Doreen asked.

Dominic grimaced. "This is nothing compared to what I've been through lately."

"I suppose you're glad to be having your last outing with Cuaifeach?"

"I'm not sure," Dominic replied. "Really, I can't make up my mind about it."

"You may before today is over," she suggested, and that, finally, made him laugh. The stirrup cups of port and brandy were emptied, the huntsman blew his horn and the field was ready to move. The field-master gestured to Dominic to come along with him.

"We'll soon have you blooded," he said with a wink, referring to the custom whereby hunting debutantes have their forehead smeared with the fox's blood.

Only Cuaifeach wasn't too keen on leaving his beloved Doreen now that he had finally found her again. In the end Bill Ryan ordered her to go into the house, out of the stallion's sight.

All the traffic on the main Dublin road stopped to let the horses pass—a hunt is traditionally given priority over other traffic. Doreen and Julia went down a small road after the horses, together with a group of other foot-followers, who seemed to know exactly where to head. They all trudged across a long field from where they had a good view of the hunt surrounding an area of dense scrub. Nothing much was happening; the riders seemed to be just standing around.

"The hounds are casting," one man explained to Doreen and added, when he saw the blank look on her face. "That means they're looking for a fox."

"Oh I hope they won't find one," the girl said. She rather liked foxes, even though one had taken all her sister's chickens not so long ago.

The man looked outraged and moved off.

"Be careful what you say here," Julia warned in a low voice. "Remember you're surrounded by enthusiasts."

One of these was an elderly lady who looked like a cosy old granny except for a network of thin blue veins on her cheeks and a grim set to her lower jaw.

"My poor little girls," she kept saying and then explained that she was referring to her two terrier bitches who had been denied a wonderful day's hunting on account of both of them being on heat.

"They were absolutely devastated when I left them in the car."

"How do terriers hunt foxes?" Doreen wondered.

"The hunt couldn't do without them!" the woman informed her. "They go where hounds can't make it, down stone covers to bolt the fox out. Thanks to them, he hasn't a chance," she added lustily.

And then she went on to tell the girl about her own darlings, how smart they were, much cleverer than the hunt's own terriers.

"Only the other day they chased a cat up a tree," she said gleefully. "And do you know, they hid under a bush nearby until the cat came down. They sat there for hours, not making a sound."

"What happened when the cat came down?" Doreen asked anxiously.

The woman smiled triumphantly. "They tore it to pieces."

Doreen turned away, as any true animal-lover would in the face of such senseless blood-thirst.

Suddenly the woman perked up. "Listen!" she cried. "The hounds are giving tongue! That means they've found a fox."

There was indeed a lot of whimpering going on in the bushes, and the next second a fox was seen running across the field closely followed by the pack and then the horses at full stretch. Cruel or not, Doreen had to admit it was a magnificent sight to see so many horses galloping together and then jumping a stone wall before disappearing out of sight. She looked for Cuaifeach, but he was hidden somewhere in the middle of the throng. She thought of him and Dominic, the thrill they must be experiencing together this minute, and felt just a little pang of envy.

The foot-followers did their best to pursue the hunt, climbing over fences, jumping streams, battling through thick undergrowth. You could tell which way the horses were going by looking at the stock in the fields. Cows usually turned their heads in the direction of the hunt, while sheep tended to flock together, out of its way.

When they finally picked them up again, the field had arrived at the second draw. Having lost the first fox, the hounds were now in the cover casting for another. Horses and riders were at a standstill once more and, judging by their bored or else restless demeanour, had been so for some time.

The sun was out, shining as brightly as it only does in the early spring, and Doreen turned her face up to feel its welcome warmth burn her cheeks.

"Isn't it lovely?" she said to the terrier woman standing next to her.

"Lovely?" the woman snapped. "It's disastrous! Sun is the last thing you want when you're hunting."

"Why?" Doreen asked.

"It dries up the scent."

On Julia's suggestion, the two of them walked on along the cover to see if they could catch a glimpse of Cuaifeach. They found him behind a hillock making amorous overtures to a huge mare, one of the seventeen-handers. On her back was a gruff-looking man in a red coat, who plainly wasn't amused.

"Oh dear!" Julia whispered. "Look at his coat. That means he's a master."

They saw him give Dominic a stern reprimand and motion with his whip for the boy to take the stallion away. Dominic tried, but in vain. Doreen sympathised with him, she knew only too well how stubborn Cuaifeach could be when he was in that mood. However, a smack on the nose from the master's whip soon shifted him.

The huntsman blew his horn to call the hounds back and go on to the next draw. The woman who owned the clever terriers explained to them that this was a good distance away and they had better do like her—go back to get their car and drive on. It took them a good hour to reach the spot the woman had described to them; it was hard to find and they got into trouble a few times on the narrow muddy track. At last they came upon the hunt standing around a cover yet again, but this time quite close to the track. Dominic and Cuaifeach were hovering on the outskirts of the field, so close, in fact, that Doreen and Julia were able to speak to them.

"He's got the hang of it now!" Dominic announced proudly. "He absolutely loves going after the hounds, he can't get enough of it! We've had some incredible gallops." He made no mention of the fact that he had been told off several times for over-taking the field-master.

Just as the hounds came out from the cover "speaking" excitedly and following a line in the high grass, a battered estate car drove up. From the furious yapping going on inside, you could tell straight away that it was the woman with the terriers. She shouted something about lying down and being quiet and then carefully opened the door to let herself out.

"I got stuck in the mud!" she complained in a loud voice. "Have I missed anything?"

Behind her back the clever terriers were jumping

excitedly on the car door trying to get out. It mustn't have been properly shut for suddenly it gave way and opened, just a crack but enough for both dogs to slink out.

"Oh my God!" the woman shrieked when she saw them disappear in a flash in amongst the hounds. "Is it dogs or bitches today?"

Before anyone had time to respond, the answer to her question was plain to see. All the dogs of the County Galway hunt took off after the two terrier bitches on heat, followed by a certain pony stallion who had "got the hang of it", in so far as he had worked out that, when hounds move, you follow. After him came those of the field who, like his rider, were not in a position to control their mounts—as it turned out, a fair number.

The whole field was in pandemonium, as if it had indeed been struck by the *cuaifeach*. The terrier-woman screamed for her darlings, the huntsman blew his horn, the field-master and some of the others galloped round to block the path of the rebels, while the clever terrier bitches dived for cover in amongst the scrub where the horses weren't able to pursue them. It was a good while before all the mounts were back under control, the hounds reluctantly returned, and the woman came bustling out of the cover, a quaking terrier under each arm.

"You ought to have known better, Mrs Sloane," the field-master told her angrily. "Really, I'm surprised at you."

"I just brought them along to watch," she

defended herself. "They've never escaped before. It's just that they so love hunting."

The master on the big mare had turned to Dominic.

"This pony has caused enough trouble for one day," he said. "You'd better take him home."

*   *   *

Later that evening Doreen and Julia relaxed with a cup of hot chocolate in front of a blazing turf fire in Raftery's Rest. Darkness was falling outside and members of the hunt were dropping in to exchange a few words and have a warming drink before going on home. The small-talk revealed that most were disappointed with their day's sport. Only two foxes had been drawn and both of them lost, one due to the incident with the wretched terriers. The sun shining fiercely all afternoon hadn't helped matters, though it had been a relief to get rid of the troublesome pony stallion....

The animal in question was now in a trailer in the car park contemplating his misdemeanours. Julia was going to take him home, but first she intended to have a word, as planned, with Bill Ryan, the field-master, who was busy going around saying good-bye to people.

Finally he joined them at their table. Julia introduced Doreen as the owner of Cuaifeach.

"Don't be too cross with him," the girl pleaded. "He's never hunted before, he really couldn't help it."

Bill Ryan dismissed the whole thing with a wave of his hand. "I felt sorry for the lad. The master was a bit hard on him. And it became downright embarrassing when the father turned up."

Roc O'Neill had joined the foot-followers just a fraction too late, brandishing an expensive video camera, with which he intended to eternalise his son's pursuits in the hunting field. Instead he had been told the boy had been banished and needed a lift home. Even Roc with his limited knowledge of fox-hunting must have figured out that this constituted a major humiliation.

Bill Ryan was watching Julia intently.

"I've been looking forward to meeting you," he said. "The brave lady who's taken on the Connemara mafia."

"That's exactly what I wanted to talk to you about," she said and got a quick smile in response, as if this was no more than he had expected.

She reminded him of his brief appearance at the Clifden social and of the cryptical comments he had made to Michael Sullivan.

"I got the impression that you didn't approve much of the 'Friends of the Connemara Pony'," she stated tentatively.

"Don't tell me they're putting obstacles in your way?" he said in mock surprise.

The waitress brought him a steaming cup of tea. Bill Ryan sipped it and then leant back and crossed his legs, obviously enjoying the comforts of the plush sofa after a long day in the saddle.

"Tell me more," he said.

Julia handed him a sheet of paper. "This was passed on to me by my customers in England," she told him.

Bill Ryan contemplated it for a good while. It was a typed letter addressed to the Longwood Riding Club in Sussex and read as follows:

Dear Sirs,

It has been brought to our attention that you have a certain Mrs O'Reilly acting for you in Connemara buying up ponies on your behalf.

We consider it our duty to let you know that she is doing your good selves, as well as the Connemara trade, a serious disservice by picking sub-standard ponies and charging inordinate amounts for them. Since we know for a fact that she underpays the sellers, it is painfully obvious that most of your money goes into her own pocket. She is, in other words, robbing you, her customers, of considerable sums of money.

We strongly urge you not to have any further dealings with this disreputable woman, who is in no way whatsoever qualified to deal in Connemara ponies.

At the same time we would like to inform you that we, the undersigned, represent a non-profitmaking group acting entirely in the interests of the Connemara pony breed. Helped by the well-documented authority of our members, we shall

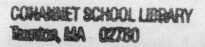

*be only too pleased to furnish you with any
number of ponies you may require.*

The letter was signed "Friends of the Connemara
Pony" and the address given was a PO Box in Dublin.

"What a bunch of dirty so-and-sos" was Bill Ryan's
reaction.

"Luckily my customers are decent people," said
Julia, "and they know me through mutual friends. So
no great harm has been done by this letter—they just
sent it straight to me."

"But how on earth," said Bill Ryan thoughtfully,
"did they get hold of your customers' name and
address?"

"By breaking into my house," Julia replied.
"Nothing was stolen, but I did notice that someone
had gone through the papers on my desk."

"And what do you think I can do to help?"

"At least tell me who they are," Julia asked. "I have
a feeling everyone in Connemara knows, but, for
some reason, no-one is prepared to talk."

"My own Uncle Christy," Doreen added, "told her
some questions are better left unanswered."

"That's to be expected," said Bill Ryan. "People
wouldn't want to fall out with this bunch. After all,
they depend on them for selling their ponies."

"They get a darned sight better deal from me,"
Julia protested.

"But they can't rely on that. You may be just a
flash in the pan. This time next year you could be
gone, and they'd be back with the regular dealers."

"So that's what they are," Julia stated grimly. "Regular dealers?"

"Of course," said Bill Ryan. "And you must understand that they are upset. You're threatening, if not their livelihood, at least a very convenient extra income."

The cast list as read out by Bill Ryan sounded like something out of a Gilbert and Sullivan opera. There was Mrs Deadly (her real name was Mrs Begley, but no-one referred to her as that). She was the leading light and Mr Bow-and-Scrape, also known as Michael Sullivan, was her henchman. Then there was Ovenpad ("Owen Paddy Ryan, no relation, I assure you!"), who had earned his nickname from a habit of always bolstering himself.

"I know him!" Doreen burst out. "He tried to get Cuaifeach off me by telling terrible lies...he's a horrible man!"

"He'll stop at nothing," Bill Ryan agreed. "And then there's another member who also has a connection with your stallion. A certain Mr Greene, aptly named for his envious nature, he doesn't even need a nickname. You both know the story of him and his court case, don't you?"

They did. Everyone in Connemara knew all about that, though by now it was many years ago.

These people and a few more like them, according to Bill Ryan, had got together to form a ring. With the trade in Connemara ponies dwindling as more and more breeders were enticed by more profitable types of farming, dealers had made a joint effort to boost their cheap source of supply. The purpose of the social in Clifden had been, on the one hand, to encourage people to go on breeding as before, and on the other hand, to track down existing breeders and their stock.

"I see!" Julia exclaimed. "That's why they insisted on taking everyone's details."

"My dad didn't like that one bit," Doreen put in.

"The price of a few free drinks was low for such a wealth of valuable information," Bill Ryan said drily. "It provided them with a comprehensive inventory on which to base future trade."

"And how do you know about all this?" Julia wondered.

Bill Ryan laughed. "I've been around horses all my life," he replied. "I learnt my lessons early. Keep to myself, get in nobody's way and depend on no-one. That would be my advice to you."

"It seems I have a lot left to learn," Julia said gloomily.

Bill Ryan looked at her, amused. "I wish I had been there that night to hear your speech," he said. "I was told about it afterwards and I couldn't stop laughing for days. There they were, thinking they were so cute, and you just stood up and snatched their custom away from right under their noses. They must have been livid! I'm surprised they haven't gone to greater lengths to stop you."

Julia told him about the phone calls and the anonymous letter. She had, incidentally, had no more trouble since the break-in.

Bill Ryan was deep in thought. "They must have a local contact out there," he said after a little while. "Someone who carries out the dirty work your end. I'm afraid I have no idea who that might be. You'll have to find that out for yourself."

Julia had a final question for him. "What exactly would you do, if you were in my shoes?"

"I wouldn't have got into them in the first place," he laughed. "But seriously, there's not much you can do. The gardaí can act only when you have direct proof against the person who did the actual breaking and entering."

"What about the Connemara Pony Society?"

"They would most likely regard the matter as a squabble between members and refuse to take sides."

Julia, who had secretly hoped that Bill Ryan would have some constructive advice to offer, was beginning to feel deeply depressed.

"I thought I was on to a good thing," she said. "Now I just wish this whole deal was over. I have to see it through, though, for the sake of the customers."

"You do of course," Bill Ryan agreed. "You couldn't possibly let these crooks win. But I'll tell you one thing: if you find yourself short of ponies, come to me. I have plenty of them, as you know. I'll fix you up."

"I could have come to you from the start," Julia said. "It would have saved me a lot of trouble. But you see, I did have some high-minded ideas of helping the smallholders who really needed the money...of doing something for the Connemara breed...."

"I know, I know," said Bill Ryan. "We were all impressed at the time. But at the end of the day, I think you'll be the one that needs helping."

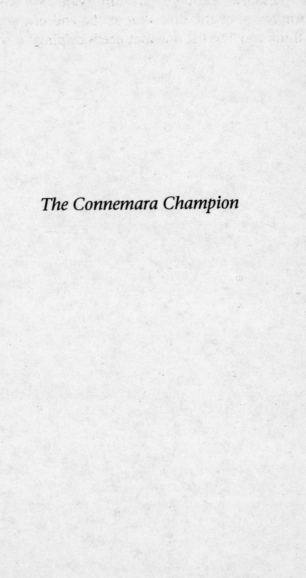

The Connemara Champion

10

Easter week saw the arrival of spring in Connemara and, with it, the first influx of tourists. The streets of Clifden were suddenly jammed, as foreign and brand-new hire-cars were added to those of the local population. On the pavements people strolled leisurely in the sunshine, caressed by a gentle southerly breeze.

No more hurrying away from wind and rain, no more diving into dark pubs for shelter! Just like the visitors, residents took their time, stopped for a chat, queued patiently in shops, where trade was showing every sign of a favourable start to the season. Up at the Square tourists took their meals at tables outside the restaurants, while the locals settled on benches to indulge in that rare brand of tranquillity that tends to take a hold of Connemara people on sunny days.

The sun was still up on Tuesdays evening, when suddenly the peace was broken. All along Market Street people stood and stared, as if they were waiting for a reappearance of the St Patrick's Day parade. At the Square benches were abandoned, curiosity one up on relaxation. Over the din of holiday traffic the rumbling of a powerful diesel engine could be heard, but with all the cars pulling in and out of parking spaces, progress up Market Street was slow.

Eventually the vehicle appeared at the Square, a huge articulated lorry some sixty feet long. It was in a condition as if it had come straight from the factory: paintwork gleaming white, chrome fittings glittering golden in the light of the setting sun. On its sides was painted in large brown letters: *Joe McGovern International Horse Transport.*

"Holy Mary and Joseph!" Paddy Pat exclaimed. "That's what I'd call a fair wagon!"

"Who on earth would be bringing so many horses to Connemara?" mused Noel Walsh, pleased to have discovered for himself what the vehicle was for.

"Don't be an eejit!" Long John snapped. "Whenever in history were horses ever brought here? Surely they've come to take some away."

The lorry had a spot of trouble turning the corner into Main Street, and matters were not much helped by the double parking of a French car outside the Post Office. Long John, always dependable, took it upon himself to direct the traffic. The Frenchman shifted, he then helped the lorry reverse from Main Street straight back onto a designated space outside the Alcock and Brown Hotel. Once in place, it took up the entire stretch of road in front of the hotel.

By the time the engine had died down, the lorry was surrounded by a group of interested onlookers, mainly locals eager to see what kind of man would emerge from such an impressive vehicle. However, when the door of the off side of the cab opened and a small, wiry figure jumped out, most faces dropped, for he was none other than Seamus Lee from Cashel, grinning delightedly at the looks of astonishment facing him in the crowd.

"Whatever got you into that contraption?" Long John inquired discreetly so as not to spoil the effect.

"He stopped for diesel at Recess," Seamus Lee whispered back. "I asked him for a lift, offered to show the way."

While the driver slipped into the hotel unnoticed, Seamus did his best to keep up the illusion that he was somehow involved in this sensational transport, holding forth as if he were in a lecture theatre, displaying an amazing knowledge, considering he had had only the short ride from Recess to Clifden to absorb it all.

"It will take thirty ponies!" he informed the gaping crowd. "Thirty ponies to England for that Englishwoman over at Errislannan!"

A man on the edge of the crowd stiffened up. He was Jim Lydon, Julia's neighbour, and now he stepped forward to Seamus Lee.

"That's not possible," he said in a strangled tone of voice.

"Oh yes it is," Seamus quipped. "He's going down there at five o'clock tomorrow morning, to avoid the traffic on these roads. The ponies will load in no time, he says, and then he'll be off to catch the midday ferry from Dun Laoghaire."

"That must have cost a fortune," one old man ruminated, thinking of the twenty pounds he had just parted with to have his mare taken to Galway in a rusty cattle trailer.

"Six thousand pound!" Seamus Lee cried triumphantly to a gasp from his audience. "Six thousand delivered in England. And that's cheap at that. She got herself a special deal, because they were going over for bloodstock from Newmarket anyway. Normally this lorry only takes racehorses. Racehorses worth millions."

People in the crowd were mumbling and shaking their heads, repeating the words "six thousand" to each other. To them it was inconceivable that anyone would pay that sort of money just to transport ponies.

"It rides like a curragh on a flat calm sea," Seamus continued when he felt they were ready for a fresh bout of information. "It's on air suspension," he pronounced carefully, aware that he was introducing them all to a brand new concept. "That means the container sits like on an air cushion so there's no swaying or bumping. And when you go through a sharp bend or up and down hills, it stays straight."

By now his audience were beginning to look sceptically from him to the lorry. Seamus was known for his propensity to exaggerate.

"The system was developed for transporting computers," he added with an air of unmistakable authority.

At this point Joe McGovern, driver and owner of the lorry, came back out. Flattered by the interest and entreated by Seamus and a few of the others, he agreed to open up the back to show off the interior. The hydraulically operated ramp was smoothly lowered and the crowd found themselves staring into a cavern of comforts such as none of them possessed in their own homes: ten roomy boxes, each with its own window just the right height to see out, non-slip carpets on the floor and straw beds so soft and fluffy you almost longed to stretch out on them. Equipment included automatic drink dispensers ("fancy having one of them at home, full of Guinness," Noel Walsh said wistfully), heating and air conditioning, as well as music playing softly to soothe raw nerves on long journeys.

"And I thought the new coach going to Dublin was luxurious," sighed Paddy Pat. "Compared to this, it's downright basic."

"I hope you're not thinking of taking this machine over to Errislannan?" somebody called out to Joe McGovern. It was Jim Lydon.

Joe looked up. "Why not?"

"You'll be stuck there for ever. Nowhere to turn and nothing but bog all around."

For a moment Joe McGovern seemed concerned. Getting stranded was a constant hazard when driving such a large vehicle. Not long ago a delivery had landed him in a dead end high up on a hilltop in Tuscany. It had taken the local fire brigade five hours to bring him down backwards.

"No problem!" shouted Seamus Lee. "He can drive in at Upper Errislannan and come all the way round. That way there'll be no need to turn round at all."

Jim looked disappointed, but Joe gave Seamus an appreciative nod. Unlike the rest of them, he seemed to think the world of this fellow. Seamus preened like a peacock.

The crowd hovered around the lorry, passing comment, asking questions, until darkness fell over the streets of Clifden. Then Julia and Doreen arrived in the company of the English customers, Mr and Mrs Harrison. They, too, were duly impressed by Joe's lorry, even though they had been better prepared for it than any of the others.

"Time to close up," said Joe to the crowd and then added with a wink, "We're all being treated to a splendid dinner in here. I wish all customers were so generous!"

Julia and Doreen sank down in the soft armchairs of the hotel lobby, while the Harrisons and Joe went to their rooms to tidy up for dinner. Julia sat impassive, not speaking a word. Her face was pale and there were dark rings under her eyes.

"Are you feeling all right?" Doreen asked her.

Her friend smiled wanly. "I feel like anyone would after being through the worst forty-eight hours of her life," she replied. "Is my hair still brown, Doreen? I imagine this is the kind of experience that will turn a person grey overnight."

"Not at all," Doreen laughed. "Come on, it ended well, didn't it? That's the main thing."

"For God's sake, don't say that!" Julia cried. "That's tempting providence. They haven't gone yet, remember."

"But we made it," Doreen insisted. "There's nothing can go wrong now."

Julia just sighed and lapsed into another deep silence, very different, Doreen reflected, from the way she had been only a couple of days before, on the Sunday when Doreen arrived to stay with her for a few days. Julia had told her proudly that all was falling into place: the Harrisons were safely installed in their hotel and all the ponies on the short-list had been checked and confirmed to be in place. She had managed to get thirty-two together in the end. Now, for the next two days, she would take the Harrisons round to view them and make their final selection.

Her only concern was that the customers might not approve of enough ponies to fill the big lorry. They had impressed upon her that a full load of thirty ponies was essential to make the transaction financially viable. The main expense was the lorry, and that price was the same whether it went over with three or thirty ponies in it.

Monday morning started well for Julia, with her own three colts being shown and instantly approved by the Harrisons. So far so good, she had whispered to Doreen, as they set off to view the others, accompanied by Ger Folan, who had been contracted to do the local transporting with his horse-box, Joe McGovern having made it clear that he would go to only one central point of collection, the ponies would have to be kept together in the two fields behind Julia's cottage, awaiting his arrival on Wednesday morning.

But then the problems started. Julia had been around to see the owners as late as the previous Friday, but now it turned out that many ponies on the short-list had become strangely unavailable. Some were said to have gone missing—"up the mountain" or something equally vague—or had been sold unexpectedly over the weekend, or else the owners had unaccountably changed their mind and were no longer prepared to part with their animal. Then there were the two brothers who demanded a thousand pounds for a gelding they had previously agreed to sell for seven hundred. Mr Harrison had walked off in disgust, saying he refused to deal with people on that basis. Some people stuck to the agreed terms, but, even so, by Tuesday evening the customers had managed to buy no more than nine ponies out of the twenty-three they had been to visit. Julia was very dejected when she and Doreen returned to the cottage.

"There's always Bill Ryan," Doreen reminded her. "He's got loads of ponies, he'll make up the numbers for you."

"But I know nothing about his prices," Julia retorted. "If he realises just how desperate the Harrisons are to fill that lorry, he may double the prices there and then. And it wasn't to deal with the likes of Bill Ryan that I started this project."

"Why has it all gone wrong?" Doreen asked.

Julia shrugged. "Some people are just determined to see me fail."

On a downcast note they set out again on Tuesday. Only nine ponies left to view, all further afield in South Connemara. But here, for some strange reason, things went better. Apparently the saboteur hadn't bothered to go south of Cashel. In a couple of hours seven ponies had been seen and bought around Carna, Rosmuc and Camus, bringing the total figure up to sixteen. Only two failed to sell that day, two small ponies belonging to a woman in Carraroe. Julia had referred to them as the "teddy bear" ponies.

"Here, at least, is one owner who won't let us down," she said as they approached the grey little cottage standing on the edge of the sea. "Of all the people I've dealt with, she was the one who made me feel I was actually doing something worthwhile."

But they arrived at the cottage to find it locked up, without any sign of life, no smoke rising from the chimney.

"Did you tell her we were coming?" Mrs Harrison asked.

"Well..." Julia replied. "She wasn't on the phone, and it was an awful long way to come, so I dropped her a postcard. I was sure that would do, she seemed dead keen to sell."

Just then a man passed by the cottage, driving a

herd of cattle.

"You won't find anyone in there," he said. "They're all in Florida."

"Florida?" Julia sounded as if she couldn't believe her ears.

He nodded. "Kids wanted to see that Disney World."

Doreen felt she must look every bit as baffled as Julia and the Harrisons.

"You know, don't you," the man continued, "that she won the Lotto? Went to Dublin to spin the wheel. Brought back sixty-three thousand pound."

"Oh," Julia said weakly. "I don't suppose she'll be selling her ponies, so."

"To tell you the truth, it would surprise me," said the man.

***

They were still fourteen ponies short when they arrived at their last port of call, their very last resort: Bill Ryan's yard in East Galway. Now Mr Harrison took over the negotiations. A seasoned dealer, he didn't let on for a moment that he was after more than one or two. "And the price would have to be right."

Bill Ryan politely showed them one pony after another and didn't bat an eyelid when the customer just kept asking to see more and more. But he was certainly taken aback when Harrison ended up offering him a sizeable lump sum for those fourteen he liked best. In his astonishment he accepted the offer straight away, and with that Julia's anguish was at an end. Besides, with his yard right on the main Dublin road, Joe McGovern would be able to collect them on his way to the ferry, with no need to bring them back to Connemara.

"I liked those ponies," said Mrs Harrison as they drove back to Clifden. "Why didn't we go to this man in the first place? We might have got all the ponies from him, saved ourselves a lot of time and trouble."

Doreen had to suppress a giggle when she saw the look of exasperation on Julia's face.

"That," she replied in a tired voice, "is something I couldn't even begin to explain to you."

The Harrisons, happy and relieved at the successful outcome of their Connemara expedition, gave them all a sumptuous dinner that night. Doreen gorged herself on prawn cocktail, steak and chips and apple pie with ice cream. It wasn't every day she was taken to a smart restaurant. Julia, on the other hand, only picked at her food, and when coffee was served, said she'd rather go back home. Although the ponies had settled well in her fields, she didn't like to be away from them for too long.

They drove back under a moon shining brightly from a clear sky and stars twinkling in the velvety spring night. Once they were off the main road, everything was so lovely and peaceful, even Julia started to relax. However, that didn't last for long. Arriving at her cottage, they heard the commotion before they had even got out of the car. The noise was not entirely unfamiliar.

"It's that wretched stallion of yours," said Julia, "kicking his door again. I suppose he can't cope with having all these strange ponies around. I just hope he won't go on all night!"

While Julia checked on the ponies in the fields, Doreen went to talk some sense into her stallion. She found him in a state of acute overexcitement; his eyes were rolling and he seemed determined to break out of his stable. Doreen managed to shut the door behind her just in time before he burst out. Then he reared up, threw his front legs over the half door and tried to squeeze through the small gap at the top.

"Whatever's the matter with you?" Doreen scolded him. "Have you gone mad altogether? Surely you seen other ponies before? It's nothing to go bananas over!"

Cuaifeach sent her a brief, despairing glance before throwing himself against the door in the hope that it would give way under his weight. The trick had worked in the past, but by now the door had been well reinforced.

Outside there was the sound of running footsteps, and then Julia's face appeared above the half door, curiously ashen in the moonlight, in fact, it looked almost green. Or was it the moonlight?

"They're gone," Julia breathed in a voice that hardly carried. "The ponies, Doreen. They are all missing."

"Are you sure?" was all Doreen could think of to

say. "Have you looked everywhere?"

Julia nodded. "Both gates have been left wide open. Someone's let them out. Oh Doreen, they could be anywhere!"

For a while they stood silently, wondering how to deal with this unexpected new development. Then Cuaifeach started to play up again.

"That's what he was trying to tell us," said Doreen. "He saw them go, that's what upset him. And now he wants to go after them. Listen Julia, I'll ride him out! He'll take me to wherever they are and we'll be able to herd them back again in time for the lorry."

Julia nodded thoughtfully. Then she told Doreen to wait while she went to get the tack. She was gone somewhat longer than expected.

"I phoned the gardaí," she explained. "They are sending the patrol out. And I'll follow you in my car."

Doreen was hardly in the saddle before Cuaifeach set off. Not hesitating for a moment, he went cross-country in a straight line, as confident as a greyhound after a rabbit. He kept to a steady trot, slowing down now and then to check, perhaps for a scent, perhaps for noises, something that his sensitive nose and ears could pick up that was out of reach to human senses. Or else, Doreen reflected, he let himself be guided by pure instinct, the stallion instinct to keep his herd together, an instinct that had helped his species survive through many thousands of years. In any case, there was no doubt that he knew where he was going, and that was just as well, for the sky had suddenly clouded over and Doreen could no longer see the ground from the saddle. If only it were morning, the girl thought to herself, then we could look for hoofmarks and dung on the ground, fourteen ponies don't just vanish, they leave traces behind. But by the time the sun went up, it would be too late. Joe McGovern's lorry would be well on the way to Dun Laoghaire to catch the ferry for which it was booked, to get to Newmarket in time to collect his next consignment....

Cuaifeach stopped to sniff a boggy patch of ground and then went round in a semi-circle to climb a bank, ending up on something that felt like a track. After a little while, Doreen heard an engine behind her and saw the track lit up by the headlights of a car. She stopped and waited for Julia to pull up behind her, heard her turn off the engine, though she left on the lights.

"Do you know where we are?" Julia asked Doreen in a low voice.

"It's Jim Lydon's place, isn't it? Whatever is he going to say when he finds it overrun with ponies in the middle of the night?"

"We'll soon know," Julia said grimly. "Let's approach with caution. Keep to the grass, so that there's no hoofbeat. I'll walk on behind you."

Cuaifeach didn't like being held up, he became agitated and suddenly put up his head to send a trembling stallion cry into the night.

"Be quiet!" Doreen warned him. "We don't want to wake Jim up!"

Then they heard muffled sounds of whinnying and whickering by way of reply.

"They are up there!" Julia said. "Hurry, Doreen, you may just get there in time!"

By the light of a thin sheaf of moonlight, Doreen cantered along on the strip of grass in the middle of the track. More neighing of many ponies could be heard as they got closer to the farm. When she turned the last corner, she saw there were lights on in Jim's house as well as in the large barn on the other side of his farm yard. Slowing down to a walk, she thought she could hear voices. Not knowing what to expect, she played safe, slid off her pony and hid behind the wall of the big barn.

"Are they all right in there?" a man's voice was heard calling.

She peeped carefully around the corner of the barn. A security light had come on in the yard and she could see Jim Lydon standing there, a vexed look on his face.

"They are just a bit worked up," said another man coming out of the barn and shutting the door behind him. "It's to be expected."

He, too, was picked up by the light beam and Doreen's heart gave a lurch when she saw him, saw the slight figure, the steel-framed spectacles and the sandy, short-cropped hair. He was a man she detested more than anyone else in the world, the man called Ovenpad, Owen Paddy Ryan, whom Bill Ryan had claimed belonged firmly in the camp of the enemy.

"Well they can't get anywhere before morning,"

Jim said smugly. "That's all that matters."

The two men started to walk together towards the house, but in the event they didn't get far. A huge dark shape came flying through the air over the farm gate and the next instant hit the ground heavily almost on top of them. It was Cuaifeach, who had no intention of lurking behind an old barn when he had business at hand—the most important business of gathering up his herd, having finally managed to locate it.

"What the hell?" cried Ovenpad.

"It's that damned stallion!" Jim shouted, making a lunge to grab hold of his reins.

"Why is he all tacked up?" Ovenpad wondered, but his question was swallowed up by the night.

Cuaifeach was furious. He didn't like strange men lunging at him on dark nights—who does?—especially not when he was about to join his herd. Ovenpad rushed up to try and catch him, but by then the stallion had decided that he had had enough and reared up angrily, brushing the man's chest with a front hoof. Terrified, Ovenpad retreated, only to find himself flat against the wall in a corner with no escape route. The beast was coming at him, ears glued back, teeth bared.

Ovenpad panicked. "Get him!" he bawled hysterically. "He's going for my throat! Get him!"

Jim ran to his aid, carrying a big shovel, which he raised in the direction of Cuaifeach.

"No!" came a shout from over at the gate. Cuaifeach and both men turned and stared as

Doreen ran into the yard and up to her stallion. In an instant she had him caught.

"Don't you lay a hand on him," she cried to Jim, who was still holding his shovel high in both hands, as if it were a ceremonial sword. "Don't you dare do anything to hurt him!"

"Get out of here!" Jim Lydon snarled between his teeth. "You and that blasted animal, get out before I call the guards. You're trespassing."

At that very moment Doreen saw the sky over the bog light up with a flashing blue light. There was no doubt about it, it was coming closer.

"You won't have to bother doing that," she said triumphantly. "They're already on their way."

***

At five o'clock the following morning the sixteen ponies were loaded quickly and efficiently into Joe McGovern's lorry, to depart at exactly twenty to six. Seeing it disappear round the bend, Julia put her arms around Doreen and unexpectedly burst into tears.

"I can't believe it," she blubbed. "It's all over. And you know, Doreen, I could never have done it without you."

Doreen, overcome by this torrent of emotion, did her best to laugh it off.

"Come off it," she said jokingly. "You know as well as I do that it was all thanks to Cuaifeach."

11

The coach travelling through Ireland on a
lovely Sunday in June might not have had the
comforts of Joe McGovern's horse transport,
but it was alive with good cheer, brimming with
laughter. The Connemara Pony Society had laid on
this day trip to the Ballinalee Show in County
Longford as part of a drive to create incentives for
Connemara-based breeders whose dwindling
numbers were a cause of concern to the Society, as to
many others. Likewise, they had arranged for Ger
Folan's lorry to bring ponies that were entered for
the various classes. With subsidised travel and meals
at reasonable prices, the offer had had an
encouraging response: both lorry and coach were
nearly fully booked.

Joe Will and Tom Samuel, the two rough-hewn
cousins from the Bens, had never been east of
Galway before. They sat in uncharacteristic silence,
staring furtively at the leafy landscape outside.

"Them fields are weird, like," Joe Will hissed to his
cousin as they passed through a particularly flat and

fertile part of the Midlands. "I mean, look at it! Not a stone in sight!"

Tom Samuel gave a snort. "People here must be mad for work," he said in a voice full of scorn. "Fancy taking away all them stones, when they would have done nicely for building walls."

It never occurred to him that other parts of Ireland might be different from his own native region.

At the other end of the scale were the veteran visitors to pony shows, headed by Marty MacDonagh, who had not only taken his pony all the way to the Dublin Horse Show, but had walked off with the championship for his beautiful mare Veronica, Cuaifeach's dam. No wonder Marty exuded confidence as he sat with his wife Bridie at the front of the coach, surrounded by his friends who, on occasions like this, all liked to share in his pride.

"It was her movement," he recalled, looking back at that glorious day many years ago. "The judges told me there wasn't a horse in Ireland could measure against my Veronica, the way she waltzed round the ring."

Most of the older men were travelling on their own. Those who had wives had left them behind: their womenfolk disliked straying too far from the hearth. It was different with the young ones, they seemed to go everywhere in pairs, even to the pub of an evening. There were a few such couples in the party. A group of teenage girls, who had come along more for the crack than for the ponies, kept to themselves at the back of the coach, giggling and smoking cigarettes, talking about the Show Disco that they would miss. The coach was due to return at seven o'clock.

Next to Marty up front was Johnny Tass, who was telling the other passengers all they wanted to know about the Ballinalee Show. There was no record of him ever having been to it, but that was the amazing thing about Johnny, he knew his facts regardless. He had his own ways and means of picking up knowledge, and if there were any gaps, he filled them in in such a convincing manner that no-one, not even himself, was able to draw a line between truth and conjecture. On the whole he lived up to his reputation as the most enlightened man in Connemara. With his well-documented knack for dispersing information, he was also frequently used by people in authority whenever they wished to transfer unofficial data to the public domain. Johnny probably wasn't aware of it, but many of the so-called confidences leaked to him off the record were actually meant for passing on. As indeed they were. Without delay.

For the moment talk in the coach centred on who was coming to Ballinalee and who wasn't. One woman expressed surprise that Christy Joyce was not amongst them, but Long John knew better.

"He be going up with his niece. Doreen is taking Cuaifeach, and they're all driving up with that Englishwoman, Sean and Roisin, too."

"That will be something!" called Seamus Lee. "The

cuaifeach hitting Ballinalee. I can't wait to see it!"

They all had a good laugh before going on to speculate about who else might be driving up privately. Marty MacDonagh, though not usually spiteful, could not resist saying, "I can think of one person who's not likely to turn up. Jim Lydon."

He had never got over the fact that once, three years ago when he was still showing Veronica, Jim's mare had beaten her into second place. Just as he had hoped, his remark turned the conversation to the man in question. "How is Jim?" people asked. "What's happening to him? Has anyone heard anything?"

Johnny Tass had. He'd heard just about everything there was to be heard on that score, and he had been waiting, patiently for him, for a good opportunity to impart this sensational knowledge to as many people as possible. Jim was awaiting trial, he told them solemnly. He was hoping for a short suspended sentence and chances were that he'd be let off lightly.

"He should be put behind bars," Marty pronounced primly. "You can't let people get away with that kind of shenanigan."

"The charge is one of larceny all right," Johnny Tass confirmed. "But he's putting up a strong defence. First and foremost, it was never his intention to steal those ponies. They were all to be released again after a few hours."

"He still took away ponies that didn't belong to him," Marty argued.

"He has a clean record," Johnny went on, "and

he'll get someone reliable to vouch for his good character...."

"That won't be easy!" cried Seamus Lee. "Nobody likes him any more. Come to think of it, no-one ever did."

Johnny Tass ignored the interruption. "More importantly," he concluded, "he insists that none of this was his idea. He was only the errand boy. To prove it, he's given out the names of the others."

This statement went down like a bomb. Mouths were gaping, eyes staring incredulously. Joe Will and Tom Samuel even stopped staring at the stoneless fields. "The rat of a man," Tom Samuel growled. Joe Will shook his head in agreement. "To be thinking of nothing but saving his own skin," he muttered.

Confident of everyone's attention, Johnny now divulged more details. What had really got to Jim, he said, was learning that Ovenpad had been released without charges. The man had smooth-talked the gardaí, admitting that, when visiting Jim Lydon on the night in question, he had noticed that there were a number of ponies in the barn, but it had never once occurred to him that they might belong to anyone other than his host. Unable to prove anything to the contrary, the gardaí had had to let him go.

"As slippery as an eel, that fellow," was Marty MacDonagh's verdict.

"I never trusted him," Paddy Pat averred. "He's the kind who be talking out the corner of his mouth all the time."

"Jim got hopping mad," Johnny continued. "He told the gardaí it was none other than Ovenpad had put him up to taking the ponies. He got so worked up, he even let slip that Ovenpad had paid him for breaking into Julia's house to go through her papers, not realising he was bringing another charge on to himself—breaking and entering."

Long John was deep in thought. "Jim always liked to be in with the big guys," he said. "The likes of us weren't good enough for him. Now see where it's landed him."

"I suppose they made him some fine promises," said Bridie MacDonagh, her voice betraying a wealth of bitter experience of pony dealers. "Promises they had no intention of keeping."

"Well he's burnt his bridges now," Johnny Tass resumed. "For he even went so far as to tell the gardaí about the smuggling operation Ovenpad was running with his friend Mr Greene."

That one raised a great many eyebrows in the coach.

Johnny nodded gravely. "Them two are no better than a pair of common thieves."

At the mention of the last two words, Joe Will and Tom Samuel jumped, but they soon relaxed again when they realised that Johnny wasn't referring to them. Everyone else was astounded. Johnny thought to himself that it was moments like this that made life worth living: seeing a crowd speechless in response to something he had said. In fairness it didn't happen too often when you were dealing with Connemara people.

Marty MacDonagh was so outraged he had had to stand up, but then he had a very special bone to pick with Mr Greene, who had once taken him to court in an attempt to gain possession of his champion mare.

"So that's what he intended to do with Veronica!" he exclaimed. "*Smuggle* her off somewhere!"

Johnny went on to tell them that the two had been at it for a long time. Mr Greene had bought some land up in Monaghan, right on the border, for the express purpose of sending lorry loads of horses on unapproved roads into the North. That way they had been able to avoid paying the VAT due on all horses and ponies entering Britain from the South. Being no less than fifteen percent of the price of each animal, the money had mounted up over the years. Ovenpad had boasted to Jim that they had cheated the Brits out of some hundred thousand pounds.

"A hundred thousand!" cried Seamus Lee. "That's more than you'd take in a bank robbery."

"Is that so?" Marty MacDonagh said drily. "I wouldn't know, it's so long since I robbed a bank."

"Why did they do it?" Paddy Pat wanted to know. "I mean, people like them who have all they want, good jobs and smart cars, fine houses, I'm sure, to live in. What was in it for them?"

"You may well wonder," said Johnny Tass. "In fact, I was having a talk the other day with that Dublin doctor who has a house over at Aillebrack, a great one for golf he is.... Anyway, he's one of them," he paused to pronounce the words syllable by syllable, "one of them *psy-chia-trists*."

"I know!" Seamus Lee called eagerly. "I know them fellows! Anything wrong with your head, they'll fix it!"

He might as well have been talking of a faulty washing machine or a broken down tractor. Johnny gave him a despairing look.

"Anyway, I asked him about it. I said, what would the reason be for two fine men like that turning to crime? Why would they want to be criminals? I asked him. And do you know? He couldn't answer."

"I think they were in it for the same reason as Jim," Long John pondered. "To prove themselves cleverer than the next man. It's a dangerous trap to fall into, but easy enough for the vain."

Everyone agreed that this was a true word spoken. Johnny Tass had to call them to attention once more, remind them that they hadn't yet heard the outcome of it all. The best bit, as he termed it.

"When the gardaí told Jim that this would be one way of reducing his own sentence, he lost no time in telling them that Ovenpad was planning to drive a lorry full of horses across the border on a certain night. That was all the information they needed. Patrols were sent out from both sides."

A deliberate pause left them all on tenterhooks.

"Well what happened? Were they caught?" Paddy Pat asked breathlessly.

Johnny smiled broadly. "Were they caught? I'll tell ye this: there be no question of them two being let off lightly. No suspended sentences there. They'll be years and years in prison."

For the first time since the coach had left Connemara, the passengers settled into a prolonged silence.

***

Ballinalee is a small village right in the heart of Ireland and as such is an unlikely setting for the only All-Connemara pony show outside Connemara, but it just goes to show what can be achieved with local initiative and great personal commitment. The show flourishes, no doubt helped by its beautiful situation in a high field outside the village, with lovely views over the surrounding counties, hills and woodland as far as the eye can see. Though mainly frequented by breeders in the East and Midlands, it also sees a fair number of entrants from Connemara itself, and never more so than this particular year, thanks to the efforts of the Connemara Pony Society.

Coming early in the season, the Ballinalee Show is chosen by many exhibitors for an idyllic first outing of the year. The results are often interesting, less predictable than those later on in the summer, when ponies are well established and winners can be picked even before entering the ring.

The show is also popular amongst owners of ridden ponies. The juvenile riding class is a qualifier for the All-Ireland Ridden Championship and there is an open class for adult riders. Moreover, there is an excellent working hunter course, the only one in the country exclusive to Connemara ponies. A rare opportunity for the tough, athletic little horses of the western seaboard to show what they are really capable of.

It was in fact mainly for the working hunter class that Doreen had brought Cuaifeach to the show. Not that she had ever attempted such a course before—nor had her pony for that matter. But there's a first time for everything, she reckoned, and it was the only chance they were going to get that summer.

They had arrived late, having underestimated the state of the roads in inland Ireland, which were not much better than those in the West. In fact, they were only just ahead of the parade, another special feature of the Ballinalee Show that traditionally marked the opening. Over a dozen floats, horse-drawn carts, traps and carriages, some coming from as far afield as Leitrim and Mullingar, filed first through the village street and then on a mile or so along the road to the show ground, where they did two laps of the main ring before stopping to be admired, inspected and judged. Amongst those competing for the awards this time were cowboys and indians, a king and queen, a couple of formidable dinosaurs and one man in a pram dressed up as a baby.

The judges were usually the same every year, one of them the secretary of the Connemara Pony Society, but she had been unable to come on this occasion and instead the Department of Agriculture had sent along a person whom they referred to as "the official authority on Connemara ponies", a man who had recently delighted his superiors by presenting them with an immaculate, comprehensive report on the pony population in Connemara. Though sporting a bowler hat specially purchased for the occasion, his tall, lean figure was instantly recognised by the Connemara crowd. They'd seen enough of him in months past. He was, of course, Wilfrid Smith-Andrews.

While the floats were being judged, Doreen busied herself getting her pony ready for the first riding class, which was due to take place immediately after the parade. She spent some time brushing him down; he normally travelled very well but it was a hot day and he had sweated up in the trailer. Julia was standing right behind her talking to Ger Folan, and, as she worked, Doreen picked up snippets of their conversation. Was Julia looking for more ponies to buy? Ger wanted to know. Oh no, was the answer. She was finished with all that. From now on she'd concentrate on her painting. That was a great pity, said Ger, for she'd been doing a grand job, to benefit many people. Julia said that had indeed been her aspiration, but she considered herself defeated. She wasn't going to fight dragons any more, it was waste of time. Not at all, Ger protested. Her work had brought about great changes in Connemara. People had got their eyes opened.

Suddenly Doreen realised that they had stopped talking. She had a feeling she was being watched.

Glancing up she found that Julia had gone off somewhere and Ger was looking Cuaifeach up and down. Meeting her eyes, he smiled benignly.

"That horse never looked better," he said approvingly.

Ger was right. Being cosseted in a smart Dublin stable with plenty of good food and hard work had left Cuaifeach superfit at the end of the winter, when most ponies were at their lowest. The new spring grass on top had added extra splendour, so that now he looked as if he was about to burst with good health. Bone he had always had; now his muscles bulged under the sparkling coat, hard and strong, covered with just enough fat to give him a lovely rounded outline.

"He'll do well in the stallion class," Ger went on. "I tell you, there aren't many like him at this time of year."

Doreen looked hesitant. "I don't know that we'll make it to the stallion class," she told him. "You see, the working hunter class is on in the other ring, and they look like clashing."

Ger frowned and looked very serious for a moment. Then he said, "Listen, my girl. Will you take a piece of advice from an old man who's got your best interests at heart?"

"Of course," Doreen replied, smiling.

"Then forget this working hunter nonsense. Go for the stallion class. No riding. Do you understand?"

Doreen looked at him, aghast. "But it's the riding I like, it's the jumping I came for! Cuaifeach is hopeless in hand."

She had only ever shown him in hand once, at the Roundstone Show when he was four, and she had promised herself it was never going to happen again. He had been so naughty, instead of standing up for inspection, he had thrown himself on his back and rolled, as if he believed it was his belly they wanted to inspect. Then he stood up, shaking mud and sand all over the judges. When told to walk away from the judges, he had turned round and emptied his bowels right in front of them, to hoots of laughter from the spectators, and finally, while trotting back towards the judges, he had taken off at a gallop. Doreen, holding on, had never run so fast in her life. Neither of them saw where they were going: Doreen narrowly missed crashing into one of the judges, while Cuaifeach went for the other. Terrified, the judges had to run for cover in a most undignified manner. It was hardly a way to endear yourself to the powers that be. Predictably, they were placed last.

Ger still looked very thoughtful.

"Why?" Doreen demanded. "Why should I show him in hand?"

"I can't tell you that," Ger said. "I just wish you'd trust me. Forget the riding, just for today, Doreen. Think of your pony rather than yourself."

And with that he walked away.

Doreen left Cuaifeach with Julia and then went over to take a closer look at the working hunter course. It looked terribly exciting: gates, ladders and wheelbarrows to jump, a tree-lined tunnel and a rick of turf, eleven fences in all. It wasn't that she had any illusion of winning—chances were they wouldn't even get around the course. But it would be such fun to try it. It would be good for Cuaifeach, too. He loved this kind of thing. Didn't he?

She found Julia and Cuaifeach joined by Wilfrid, who had completed his task for the day by awarding a nice cup to a Tyrannosaurus Rex, an animal far less intimidating than the stallion, to whom he kept a respectful distance, at least he attempted to, but Cuaifeach kept sidling up next to him, and Wilfrid had to move round and round in a circle to get away from him. It made you dizzy just to watch them.

"Can you understand what he meant?" Doreen asked Julia after relating what Ger Folan had advised her.

Julia couldn't. "He's probably right, though," she said. "Ger wouldn't say something like that without a good reason."

"Of course he wouldn't," Wilfrid added. "You should do as he suggests."

Wilfrid had an annoying habit of always going along with Julia, buttering her up, as it were. Doreen wondered whether this was somehow connected with the fact that Julia insisted on keeping their relationship platonic. Perhaps he thought she would change her mind and fall in love with him if he kept agreeing with her at every turn.

"But why did he say I should be thinking of my pony?" Doreen went on. "I mean, I never think of anyone else."

Julia's reply was lost as Wilfrid suddenly clutched Doreen for support. Cuaifeach had given him a playful push that had very nearly knocked him over. He straightened himself up and adjusted the bowler hat. It was a size or two too large and tended to fall down over his ears.

The first riding class was called.

With a determined set to her chin, Doreen picked up her saddle and put it on Cuaifeach's back. He put his ears back and glared at her, and when she bent down for the girth, he turned his head and gave her a painful nip in the back. The bridle he avoided by sticking his nose right up in the air.

"Don't you start!" the girl cried. "I have enough with the others!"

Cuaifeach snorted and gave her a defiant look. Doreen resolutely reached up to force his head down, but then he took a giant leap sideways, landing heavily, as it happened, on Wilfrid's foot. The poor man's face went white under the brim of the bowler hat. Then it contorted, as he tried desperately to be brave. Doreen felt sorry for him. She, too, had been stood on by horses and she knew that, while it rarely caused any serious injury, the initial pain was horrendous. Julia led her badly limping friend over to where the ambulance was parked, and Doreen found herself abandoned, without anyone to help hold the stallion, who was determined not to be tacked up.

They battled for a long time. There was no sign of

Julia. When Doreen realised she had missed her class, her determination suddenly left her. What was the point, she asked herself. Why go on, if it was a losing battle anyhow? Exhausted, she put down the saddle.

"All right then," she muttered. "You win. You all win. I've come all this way for nothing."

She put the pony back in the trailer and sank down on the straw in front of him. Cuaifeach was a heart-breaker, Dominic had said, he probably couldn't help it, it was just the way he was made. Dominic was doing very well at present on the new jumping pony his father had bought him, he had even won a class against the clock at the Spring Show in Dublin.

"The key to it is to have a decent pony," he had said when they last met. "I don't know why I ever bothered with that hoodlum from Connemara."

Doreen had said nothing in reply. The key to it, she thought, is to have a rich daddy.

While Cuaifeach felt rather pleased with life, having had his way plus a nice net of hay to munch his way through, Doreen spent the early part of the afternoon sulking in the trailer. She had no wish to watch the riding classes she should have been in and dreaded meeting her parents and uncle Christy and having to explain to them what had gone wrong, why she wasn't out there enjoying the working hunter course. When she finally went out, she made straight for the in-hand arena, searching out some of the Connemara people she knew. As usual they were chatting amongst themselves, disappointed, it transpired, that not a single pony from Connemara had as yet won a class. Marty MacDonagh said it was too early in the year for their ponies, it took longer for them to pick up after the winter. "Just wait till August," he said, "that's when we'll be showing them all."

Doreen asked Johnny Tass what the present class was.

He informed her that it was Class Six, for two-year-old fillies, and Mrs Deadly's pony, led by Bow-and-Scrape, alias Michael Sullivan, had been pulled in first in the preliminary line-up. Mrs Deadly had come all the way from Waterford only because she knew one of the judges tended to favour her ponies. She only ever went to shows where she knew a judge to be favourably inclined. Funnily enough, the two judges today didn't seem to have many views in common, they had been seen arguing non-stop. Perhaps Mrs Deadly wouldn't win the show after all.

"Sshhh," somebody warned him, pointing to the lady in question, who was stationed not far from them. She was a woman with a sharp, lined face, and she was watching the proceedings in a state of extreme tension, as if her very life was at stake. Teeth clenched, she stared from her overconditioned, overexcited filly to Michael Sullivan, as the former played up and the latter gave every impression of having taken on more than he could comfortably handle. However, ten minutes later, she relaxed noticeably, when the red rosette was handed over.

She even rushed up to the ring to snatch it from Sullivan, together with the prize money.

"We can all relax now," said Johnny with a wink. "There'll be no rows, no complaints about rigging, no throwing back of minor rosettes in the judges' faces. Mrs Deadly's day is saved, and ours with it."

"Don't speak too soon," warned Seamus Lee. "She's yet to take the championship."

Doreen missed most of this, for she had gone back to get Cuaifeach. The stallion class was next on the agenda. She found him with his head covered in hay, like a long blonde wig, but that was soon brushed off, and then they hurried down to the ring. It was always a good idea to be in early, it caught the judges' eyes.

Ropes had been erected to separate the crowd from the stallions. There were already three animals in the ring, led by men, big beefy fellows striding out pompously, rattling their chains. Cuaifeach had no chain, he was wearing his ordinary bridle which he had, incidentally, been quite helpful in putting on and, apart from a lunge line clipped from one ring of the bit and run through the other, Doreen had none of the usual equipment for showing stallions, she did not even carry a stick. It suddenly occurred to her that what she had might not be sufficient, but that was too late to worry about now.

Cuaifeach, who had got rather bored standing in the dark trailer, was pleased to be out and about, walking around a show ring in front of a lot of people without even having a rider on his back nagging him to do now this, now that. As far as he could tell, there were no fences to jump either. His outing was purely for pleasure.

As he relaxed, his stride became extended and more vigorous, covering a lot of ground. The rounded muscles on his back worked in a steady comfortable rhythm, the strong neck arched and the head, poised and alert, nodded in perfect balance. The dynamic movement seemed to spring effortlessly out of his powerful body, like an irrepressible natural force that would just go on and on until the end of time.

While Doreen struggled to keep up with him, he was being closely observed by one of the judges. When did I ever see a pony move so freely? he thought. It's like hearing music, watching a dolphin at play, a dove in flight. Then he remembered. It was in Dublin, when he had awarded Veronica the championship. Could this pony be related to her, he asked himself. He didn't know. Like any good judge, he hadn't seen the catalogue beforehand.

Of the eleven stallions in the ring, there were five or six of superior quality. But of those only one had exceptional movement and, as far as this judge was concerned, that settled the matter. He said as much to the other judge, the one who liked Mrs Deadly's, or more correctly, Mrs Begley's ponies. Not surprisingly, the man held a different view.

"I don't like bay stallions," he said dismissively.

"What nonsense is that?" the first judge hissed. "Whenever were we instructed to judge ponies on the basis of their colour? A child of five could do that, as long as he's not colour blind."

"He hasn't enough condition, anyhow," the other judge persisted.

"We're not here to judge the amount of fat of each animal either," the first judge said. "If that were the case, a weighing-scale would do a better job of it."

"I still prefer to award the biggest stallion," the other judge persisted.

The first judge was on the brink of despair. It had been going on like this all day, and it was getting on his nerves.

"Look at that muscle!" he growled. "That's a working stallion, as opposed to a fat slob. It's how they should look. Not to mention his movement."

The other judge, having had his way in the previous class, finally gave in and reluctantly agreed to have Cuaifeach called in first. Amazed, Doreen took up her position above all those big men. Cuaifeach was unperturbed, he looked as if he had never expected to end up anywhere else.

He managed the individual inspection very well too, standing patiently, oozing pride and confidence, while they looked him over and then walking and trotting majestically, throwing them the odd glance of regal acknowledgement. Even the long wait while the others were being judged he accepted with equanimity. When it came to the final line-up, no-one but Doreen was surprised to see him win.

They left the ring, Cuaifeach with the bright red rosette attached to his bridle, Doreen clutching the cup and her winnings, and were met by a huge cheer from the Connemara crowd, excited shrieks from Christy, delight written all over her father's face, and the voice of her mother crying, "at last we got some joy out of that horse!" Julia hugged her and said Cuaifeach had been great, with Wilfrid adding that the judging was very fair. Then Julia took Cuaifeach over to give Doreen a rest before the championship class, which was due in about an hour.

"The Championship!" Doreen exclaimed. "God help me, do I have to go into that as well?"

Her parents, hearing that she hadn't had a bite to eat all day, took her off to the tent for tea and sandwiches, and she told them how Ger had advised her not to go into the riding classes.

"He knows, of course, what a mess Cuaifeach makes of them," she said. "He must have realised he stood a good chance of winning. Aren't I glad now I listened to him?"

The time came for the Championship. All the winners paraded around the ring, watched intently by judges and crowd alike. This, of course, was the most important class of the day. The prestigious Blacksmith Trophy, commemorating the famous Irish general Sean Mac Eoin, "The Blacksmith of Ballinalee", was the one that counted.

Cuaifeach's good humour persisted, as did his good behaviour; the two usually went hand in hand. He walked around the ring with the air of one who has eventually found his right element. The same couldn't be said about Mrs Deadly's filly who, tired and overwrought after her long day, tugged at her lead and tossed her head impatiently. Michael Sullivan, painfully aware of Mrs Deadly's cold eyes on him, hit the pony with his stick, whereupon she jumped up and knocked him on the nose, causing it to bleed profusely. With both hands required to keep the filly under control, he couldn't do anything to stem the flow, but had to walk on with blood pouring down over his shirt-front. Furious, Mrs Deadly rushed into the ring and took over the pony.

"Can't you do the simplest thing," she snapped, "without messing it up?"

Michael Sullivan sheepishly stumbled out, a handkerchief pressed to his nose, while the filly, confused and unhinged by the sudden change of escort, became even more unmanageable. Mrs Deadly kept looking sternly at the judge she knew, as if she was wondering what was taking him so long. Finally her pony was called in, but so was Cuaifeach, by the other judge. The other ponies were told to leave the ring, and then the arguing resumed in earnest.

Seamus Lee couldn't resist shouting, in the loud voice that would carry across a bog: "Give the trophy to the one that catches thieves!"

The glance Mrs Deadly awarded him could have left no-one in doubt as to how she had got her nickname.

The judges could not agree, and in the end the referee had to be called in. He turned out to be none other than Ger Folan. It took him exactly five seconds to settle the matter, though he spun it out for half a minute, for appearance's sake.

Cuaifeach was the Champion of the Ballinalee Show.

Mrs Deadly did not wait for the reserve champion prize. She stomped out of the ring, hauling the poor filly behind her, and people quickly stepped aside, afraid, as it were, of crossing her path.

Pure ecstasy reigned in the Connemara camp. Cuaifeach was hailed as a king.

"That I would live to see the day!" Christy cried, his eyes brimming with tears.

"This will be a story to bring home," Johnny Tass mused contentedly.

"We're proud of you, my girl," said Sean Joyce.

"You're not without your part in this," Wilfrid whispered to Julia.

A journalist from the local newspaper came up to Doreen, accompanied by a photographer.

"How does it feel?" he asked her. "A young girl like you, to be the owner of a Connemara Champion?"

"It doesn't feel much at all," Doreen replied with a laugh. "You see, to me he's always been a champion."